BALTAIR

A TIME TRAVEL ROMANCE

JANE STAIN

Renfaire Druids (Renaissance Fair, Festival, Man)

Druid Magic (Tavish, Seumas, and Tomas)

Celtic Druids (Time of the Celts-Picts-Druids)

Druid Dagger (Leif, Taran, Luag)

Meehall

Ciaran

Baltair

Time of the Fae

See **Jane Stain's Amazon page** for more.

As Cherise Kelley:

Dog Aliens (a cuddly dog story with a happy ending)

High School Substitute Teacher's Guide

Paperback **ISBN:** 9781792174032

CHAPTER ONE

Ellie heard the door unlatch, even if the hinges were too well-oiled to make noise when it opened. Heart pounding, she scooped the loosened book page off the library desk and hid it in a drawer she had kept open for just this purpose. It was night-time, so no light came in through the stained glass windows to penetrate the shadows down by the drawers. It should be safe there.

Nadia had reached out to do the same thing.

Their hands met, and Ellie's favorite coworker was now staring at the old ring Ellie had found here and put on her right hand a few hours ago.

The white druid robes on Celtic University's librarian billowed as she strolled past their desk on her way further into the stacks, acknowledging Ellie and Nadia with a brief nod of her grey head.

Whew.

Unlike the heart-pounding panic Ellie felt at almost being caught with the book page, she felt no guilt at all about putting the ring on and making it hers. She'd found it quite by accident, covered in a thick layer of dust. Who knew how many decades (or even centuries?) it had lain on the cold stone floor behind the old wooden shelves? Perhaps it had been dropped there before all of these ancient tomes were shelved.

Ellie and Nadia hoped these old books would help translate the ancient Gaelic book pages Nadia had smuggled to the present from the past. The book pages they had not handed over to the druids. "The book was destroyed," they had told the druids. It hadn't been a lie. Not technically.

Trying not to draw Mrs. Echols' attention to the ring, Ellie picked at it with her thumbnail as if it had something caught in it, then turned to look at the books which were still on the desk.

Nadia smiled back and did the same.

Ellie's finger itched, and she twisted the ring to scratch it. Even though Mrs. Echols had nodded casually and passed by, Ellie was worried. She needed to talk to Mrs. Echols, or the woman was going to be suspicious. It was after normal working hours. Ellie and Nadia were clerks here at Celtic University, and while Nadia did take a dance class every semester, she wasn't considered an academic student who had a reason to be in the library late at night.

Ellie got up and briskly walked down the stacks the way the librarian had gone until she found her.

Mrs. Echols wasn't doing anything much, just dusting the old books. A task far beneath her station.

Surprising herself, Ellie was proactive. "You're wondering what we're doing here, aren't you, Mrs. Echols. Well, I'll tell you. It's no secret that the way to get promoted is to do extra work. Nadia's idea was writing those articles for the historical society, but let's face it. That's not going to do it. I had a much better idea. We're cataloging the ancient texts here in the stacks."

Mrs. Echols looked surprised and pleased, tucking her chin down and examining Ellie from head to toe before meeting her eyes. "That's sweet o' ye, Ellie. Do ye lasses need help?"

Hoping Nadia had heard and was coming up

with a quick catalog paper for the texts on the table, Ellie gave Mrs. Echols a self-satisfied smile. "Not yet, but I'll let you know if we do. And this won't interrupt our normal duties. As you can see, we're doing this after hours, on our time." And then unable to resist the opportunity to make a joke, she added, "Of course, we wouldn't turn away pay for this, if you offered."

Mrs. Echols raised an eyebrow. "Dinna push yer luck, Ellie."

This was accompanied by such a knowing look, that Ellie merely nodded before turning around and hightailing it back to her and Nadia's table. Whew. Nadia had heard, and the "catalogue" was well underway by the time Ellie sat back down.

Mrs. Echols passed them by again on her way out, then closed the door behind her, leaving the two of them once more in blissful solitude.

Ellie looked to her friend for congratulations on her quick thinking, ready to brush it off as nothing. Putting on some attitude, she put her hands on her hips and cocked her head to the side. "Well, did I tell her, or what?"

But Nadia was looking at Ellie's new ring with concern. When she saw that Ellie had noticed, Nadia looked the other way. "Oh, come on, Ellie.

One of these days, your jokes are going to get you in big trouble."

Ellie pointedly got the loose book page out of the drawer. Nadia's concern was silly. "People keep telling me that, but so far it's all been hysterics."

Nadia rolled her eyes.

They once more set to translating this strange Gaelic the page was written in.

When the campus bells played the midnight tune, they put on their coats, put the texts away, carefully tucked the book page from the past up into Nadia's shirt, and went out onto the dark cobblestone streets of the druids' colony, cleverly disguised as a university. There were even students, currently asleep in the dorms. The druids' deception was elaborate.

Two kilted highlanders they knew, Baltair and Eoin, awaited the women in the usual dark spot between the gas lamps in front of the history building. This time, the men had gotten wise and not brought any horses with them from 1706, for their usual midnight meeting to check on the status of translating the book Nadia had stolen from the druid child, Tahra, back in Baltair's time.

Sour-faced as usual, Eoin handed Ellie a note. Because they were inside an institution run by druids who could listen magically, they only communicated sensitive information in writing.

Nadia leaned over Ellie's shoulder and read along, silently.

Eoin's note said, "How's the translation going? Have you found out anything about how we can cure Ciaran?"

Nadia lost all trace of happiness from her face and frowned up at Eoin. "Ciaran is still ill, then? He's not getting better?"

Eoin's face grew angry. "He's worse. I'm giving you two more days, and then I'm doing what I originally promised."

Nadia took a deep breath and made fists, giving every sign she was ready to attack the huge Highlander.

Ellie grabbed her friend, stopping her. But surprising herself, she turned to Eoin and gave him a piece of her own mind. "You're the one who warned us to keep quiet out here. Now let's watch ourselves, lest the decision be taken from us. Remember where you are and what those who run this place can do."

Ellie whirled and led Nadia away, but not before she noted the lingering frost between Eoin and Nadia. Again unable to resist joking, she said to her friend about Eoin, "Doesn't he remind you of the Incredible Hulk, sometimes?"

Nadia snorted.

Baltair's eyes, though? They showed nothing but amusement. He even winked Ellie goodbye, sending her into a happy sleep.

* * *

"We're in the right," Ellie insisted to Nadia on their way to the dining hall the next morning. "We'll see a sign of it soon. We're coming close to a breakthrough. I can feel it in my bones." The joking side of her erupted into song at the top of her voice, startling passersby. "Can you feel it? Can you feel it?"

Nadia's laughter was grudging as she tugged Ellie over to where a bunch of flyers always hung on a nearby column. "Look!"

Ellie looked where Nadia was pointing, slightly annoyed that her friend was so flighty. But then she stopped and stared at the flyer. "Harold Cochran's in town?"

Nadia's voice came over Ellie's shoulder. "Yep. Just the man to help us translate an old Gaelic text. He's signing his new fantasy novel at that funky

Speculative Fiction bookstore tonight. Let's go see if he can help us."

That night at midnight, they had much better news written out for Baltair and Eoin. "We saw a flyer that said the famous fantasy author Harold Cochran was in town, signing at a bookstore, so after work we went over there. He's this big burly man, older, with a beard. And he's from the past. We both saw the signs. He keeps his distance from everyone and always keeps his weapon arm free."

Eoin grew impatient and stopped reading. "What was so great about meeting this ancient scholar? There's plenty of ancient scholars already here at this university, and we should be—"

Ellie cut him off, and that surprised her, because he was a big man. Usually, she felt quite intimidated by him, but not right now. "Keep reading."

They all read silently over his shoulder.

"We showed him Tahra's book, and you should've seen his face. His eyes went wide, and his jaw dropped open. 'Where did ye get this, lassie?' he asked us. We fibbed, of course, and told him we got it in the archives at Celtic. But he wasn't fooled. He was smart enough not to say anything about it in front of everyone around, but he didn't believe us. What he said next floored us, though. 'This is my book. I can prove it tae ye.' He grabbed the pen he had been signing his books with and wrote on the back of his business card, then held the card next to Tahra's book in Nadia's hand so we could see it was the same handwriting. He had written, 'I wrote this book. Give it back."

Eoin stopped reading again, turning his furious face on Nadia. "You know Ciaran's life depends on that book. Tell me you didn't—"

Ellie was getting used to the idea of keeping Eoin in his place. She had never tried it before last night, and she liked cutting him off. She exaggeratedly pointed to the note in his hand. "Keep reading."

They all turned to read some more of it.

"I told him he could have his book back if he translated it for us."

Ellie crossed her arms and smiled at Eoin, daring him to tell her that hadn't been a good trade.

Nadia pointed to their note, clearly impatient for them to finish reading so they could all get back to finding out how to cure her husband.

They continued reading.

"Here's the weird part. Harold just laughed and picked up one of the fantasy books he was signing. 'All that ye ask aboot is in here, lass.'"

Eoin and Baltair both looked to Ellie.

She handed them each a copy of Harold's book and showed them she and Nadia each had their own copy. "Written by Ràild MacEacharna. Clever, wasn't it, using his Gaelic name as his pen name and his English name as his civilian name in what for him is the future?"

With the awe of someone who has never before seen a mass-produced book, Baltair took the paperback in his hands and examined it closely, turning it sideways to look at how the pages had been fastened to the spine, opening it to the middle to examine how tightly it was bound, and finally squinting at the type. Finally looking up at Ellie, he nodded his agreement, drinking in her eyes with his.

Oddly, Ellie didn't get lost in Baltair's eyes. She was able to speak. Imagine that. "We're halfway through reading this book, and it's promising. You should read it before you meet us tomorrow night. The author's meeting us back at the bookstore tomorrow. If we're convinced this is adequate, then we're doing as he asked."

Still trying to be in charge, Eoin asserted, "But that doesn't give us a chance to tell you whether we are convinced or not."

Nadia raised her hand to stroke Eoin's arm (and his ego).

But Ellie'd had enough of Eoin's presumptiveness. Grabbing Nadia and turning the two of them around toward their dorm, she called out over her shoulder in a silly sing-song voice, "That's right."

Accompanied by Nadia's soft singing in the next room, Ellie stayed up most of the night reading. Despite Harold Cochrane's gruff manner, Ellie loved the man's fantasy book. She'd read many such books, and it was a rare one indeed that made you love everything about it: the characters, the magic system, the world the author had created, and the story itself. She felt she was right there with Ryan MacGregor, riding through the faerie woods with all the leaves falling around him as he raised his faerie axe and called out to his enemies.

* * *

The wind whipped Ryan's cloak against the night sky as he crested the craggy mountain. Below lay the enemy's encampment. The naked eye wouldn't be able to see it, but the faerie axe brought it all into full focus. Ryan counted five hundred warriors lying in wait below. Monstrous machines of war waited too. He could hear the enemy.

"They will expect us to form ranks."

"We will not meet their expectations."

"We'll attack with the war machine."

"And rush them while we do."

"They won't know what hit them."

When he was sure he knew the plan, Ryan rode back down the mountain to the McGregor camp. Gloating was dishonorable, so he tried not to, but the knowledge he had gained must have shown on his face, because his ride back into his clan's camp was triumphant, with everyone greeting him and cheering.

They knew—

—that he knew—

—what they needed to know.

So all was good in their world. He huddled close with them around the fire telling what he knew. And then it was to sleep for all, so that everyone would have the strength they needed on the morrow.

The faerie axe spoke to him in the night. "Would a mist help you out, do you think?"

"You know it would," he told the axe amusedly.

"Then a mist you shall have. How thick should it be?"

"So thick that the enemy doesn't see us coming."

At the very crack of dawn, Ryan was up, armored and mounted, carrying the faerie axe over his shoulder. The other men were mounted soon after, and they all nibbled on bread as they quietly rode toward the enemy camp. No one spoke. Their strategy was absolute silence.

But the faerie axe spoke to Ryan in his mind. "How grateful are you that I came to you, there in the woods?"

Ryan knew better than to tell the axe the whole truth, better than to think the whole truth, when he had the axe upon him. The fae were not to be trusted, and this was their magic in the axe, after all.

He kept his thoughts superficial and immediate. "I'm very grateful indeed that you have risen this mist around us. I suspect you're keeping us extra quiet as well, keeping the horses from snapping any twigs. I thank you greatly."

It was true. The clan's movement was unnatu-rally silent. Eerie.

When they drew near, Ryan raised his hand for everyone to stop. Everyone did, including the next greatest warrior in the group, John, who looked to Ryan, waiting for the signal to attack.

Ryan gave the signal, and everyone vaulted into action, the horses jumping over the brush to get to the enemy fast enough. Now the warriors hooted and hollered, calling out their war cries.

"For our honor!"

"MacGregor despite them!"

But the enemy warriors were up and about when the MacGregors arrived. Armed and armored, if not mounted, they had formed a large clump that would be difficult to penetrate. Had pikes up to fend off the horses.

"The mist is hindering you now, is it not?" asked the faerie axe.

"Aye, it is."

"Then it shall dissolve. My goal is to please you."

True to the faerie axe's word, the mist dissolved, allowing Ryan and his MacGregor clan to see the evil clump of the enemy in the center. Those were definitely pikes facing outward.

The axe allowed Ryan to see past them, all the way to the cliff they had camped near, with their terrible war machine perched on it, aimed at the McGregor camp. The enemy had meant to blast the MacGregors away as soon as the light came and they were able to see. The mist had saved Ryan's people.

With a holler of his own, Ryan gave the signal for everyone to charge at the enemy. 'Force them back,' his signal said. 'We have the superior force. We will make them fall off the cliff. Let's end this.'

'End it' the MacGregors had. Though enemy

pikes, impaled horses, and men alike, more horses trampled the enemy. Pushed them back, and back again, until the remainder of them went over the cliff.

The enemy was no more.

CHAPTER TWO

Baltair tried to stay stone-faced and keep his distance. He couldn't encourage the beautiful ginger Ellie to love him. It would be wrong. Ciaran and Nadia were devastated as a result of Ciaran's curse, and he might just die in the foretold epic battle against the Camerons.

But he would encourage Ellie to leave this druid compound and make her living elsewhere. This compound of many castles was evil. He could feel it emanating up from the very cobblestones of the street. Well, maybe not evil. But it reeked of danger and intrigue. It was so much more than the place of learning it claimed to be. That much he knew from his cousin Eoin, though the man attempted to keep silent.

He put his hand on the pommel of his sword when he saw a man approaching on the dark deserted avenue between the druids' huge castle-like buildings. He relaxed a bit when he saw it was an older man, but he kept alert. The man was wearing white robes, so he was one of them.

Baltair called out to his cousin, "Eoin, we have a visitor."

The old man looked straight into Baltair's eyes as if he had something to say, but then he turned and walked up the steps of the building Nadia and Ellie called 'The History Building.' After unlocking the door with a key, he went inside and closed the door behind him.

Baltair looked to see Eoin's reaction.

His cousin shrugged and inclined his head toward the library building.

Baltair looked that way to see the lasses coming.

Ellie and Nadia had obviously approved the translation of the book, because they were both bright faced and happy as they approached the usual meeting place in the middle of the night.

And Baltair knew the lasses planned on coming back to 1706 with him and Eoin, because they now wore long plaid dresses from his time. On their backs were leather satchels exactly like the one

Sarah had when she came back to 1706. Meehall said the thing was full of awes and wonders: A light that flashed brightly, blinding enemies at night. Small sticks that made fire when rubbed against something bumpy. A tiny mirror that could fit in the palm of one's hand. Pills that prevented death by fever.

Aye, Ellie and Nadia planned on going with them.

Baltair turned to Eoin then, gauging his cousin's reception to the idea.

Eoin shrugged one shoulder, indicating he didn't really care one way or the other.

Baltair and Eoin had read the book, too, of course. Much of it was silly, all the parts about the faeries and the faerie axe. But the book did give an indication of how the decisive battle between the Murray clan and the Cameron clan was supposed to go.

From the druid child's version of the book, written in an archaic form of Gaelic they could only partially understand, they had been able to figure out the battle was supposed to happen in just a few days. Now, by reading Ràild MacEacharna's English version of the book, they had an idea how many warriors the Camerons had, and where they would be. Baltair and Eoin knew the exact spot described. They would be ready.

Meehall's voice bellowed down the street, making all four of them turn their heads abruptly. "Eoin! Wait for me!"

Eoin didn't look happy to see his oldest brother. "What are you doing here?"

Baltair understood. Meehall was married now and had responsibilities. "Where is Sarah? You didn't leave her back at Murray castle by herself?"

Meehall was close to them now and smiling at the lasses in a way that didn't suit a married man.

Contempt welled up, and before Baltair realized what he was doing, he had inched closer to Ellie. He knew he had no right to claim her as his own, but he would protect her from the advances of a married man. That much was certain.

Eoin —the stern no-nonsense warrior— was smiling at his wayward brother. "What brings you here?"

What Eoin said next let Baltair relax. "This is Meehall's twin, Gabriel. He calls himself Connell, now that we go into Scotland's past. They accept that name easier, as it's more manly."

The lasses looked just as relieved as Baltair felt, and they smiled up at Connell.

"Nice to meet you," said Ellie with a polite smile.

"What a pleasure," said Nadia.

To the man's credit, Connell smiled with friend-liness but kept his distance, as befitted a stranger meeting lasses for the first time.

Baltair had a grudging sense of respect for the man he'd only just resented a moment before. It reminded him of when he and Ciaran had first met Eoin, all those years ago. He looked at Connell with curiosity now.

Eoin clasped forearms with his brother, then pulled back and studied Connell while their matching kilts swayed in the night breeze on the cobblestone street. "It's clear you know we're about to go traveling. How much did the druids tell you? What do they know?"

Connell held onto his brother's forearm, causing the younger but much larger man to look him in the eye. "It's best we don't discuss it here."

Eoin nodded and held out his other arm for the rest of them. In order to time travel with him, they needed to be in contact. And Eoin was happily married, so Ellie's proximity to the man didn't bother Baltair. Not when he made sure he was next to her when Eoin's arms went around them all.

The swirling of the world didn't catch him off

guard anymore, but it was still unnerving. He was glad he had people to cling to. The dizziness was bearable when he was close to Ellie. He made himself pull away from her as soon as it subsided and they were once again near Murray camp in 1706 Scotland.

Eoin put whatever he held in his hand that allowed him to time travel back in his sporran. Baltair once more tried to get a glimpse at it, wondering what it would be. But as usual, Eoin hid it well. "Now Connell, what dae—"

Connell hollered over his younger brother's voice, staring pointedly at Eoin's sporran. "Mayhap Malina wull hold ontae yer clothes a bit, and we can gae doon tae the river, bathe, and hae a talk."

Baltair braced himself for what he knew was coming. His cousin had never been a man of reason. He only understood action. Baltair was not disappointed.

Eoin threw up his bulging arms, punching at the sky. "Yer stalling! Tell it tae me now, or sae help me, Connell, I wull take ye back tae Druidville and leave ye. Ye hae na need tae be here. We hae recent news that puts oor situation with Ciaran in hand." He begrudgingly looked toward Ellie and Nadia. "Thanks be tae the lasses."

Baltair wasn't the only one who understood what Meehall's twin was afraid of, though.

Nadia scribbled furiously in the little notebook she kept in her backpack, and all of them crowded around behind her to read what she had written in her perfect Gaelic.

"I would na put it past the druids tae hae spelled whatever ye use tae time travel, Eoin, sae that they can hear what we say. Sarah says that happened tae Tavish's parents, with the phone the druids spelled for them. Certies ye ken aboot that. Had ye forgotten?"

Baltair felt his cousin's breath calming behind him and thus knew before Eoin said anything that this was true.

Connell held out his hand toward the notebook, the friendly concern on his face contrasting against the stormy Highlands sky.

Nadia handed it over, moving around behind him with everyone else, to read what he would write.

Connell's handwriting was flowing and beautiful.

"They ken whence ye gae, and why. They also kenned I would tell ye they kenned, sae they did na explain aboot how. There is a verra good chance they are eavesdropping on ye through the device they gave ye tae time-travel with, Eoin. I canna believe ye would be careless with that, after what happened tae Uncle Dall and Aunt Ellie."

Eoin sighed deeply, but it was the heaving sigh of a warrior, not the whining sigh of a scholar.

With the battle coming up, Baltair took comfort in that.

Eoin grabbed the notebook and scrawled in it.

"So why did ye come tae us? What was sae urgent?"

Connell took it back again, and his writing contrasted so much with Eoin's that it looked like a different language.

"The family's Renaissance faire is gang wull. Tomas and Amber want all o' us tae join them there."

Eoin scowled and grabbed the notepad, then wrote in violent, stabbing letters.

"That stupid faire is Tomas's fash. The rest o' us hae real-life events tae heed. Oor cousin Ciaran was crippled by druids last week. We seek his cure. Nadia and Ellie got us a translation of the druid child's book through the author, who it turns oot is alsae a time traveler. He alsae just now visited the city near Druidville. These canna all be chance meets, we verra wull ken. Howsoever, we need tae see tae Ciaran. Oor cousin weighs maire upon us than any faire."

Connell's eyebrows shot up as he grabbed for the pad of paper.

"O' course he does. Allow me tae be a help tae ye."

In a rare show of affection, Eoin threw his arm around his brother's shoulders. "'Tis glad I am, tae hae yer help. Let us gae tae Searc, chieftain o' the Murray clan we MacGregors hae joined, and tell him all we ken o' the upcoming battle." In barely a whisper, Eoin added, "He kens, but nay one else in the clan does save for my wife, Malina, and her son, Rory."

They walked toward the din of the Murray clan, camped out in the warlike style of the Highlanders. They were too far to hear many distinct sounds, just a general hubbub of activity punctuated by the occasional neighing of a horse or the laughter of a child.

Ellie had her arm around Nadia and changed the subject, speaking to her friend softly and with assurance. "Ciaran makes a good fantasy hero, ye ken. That determination and loyalty read wull in the pages o' the book. Betimes I found myself wishing I kenned the man, forgetting that I already did." She chuckled in that way she always did after making a jest, which she did often.

Nadia looked at Ellie with gratitude. "I had verra much the same experience. I'm lucky tae hae him, even with the crippling druid curse o' the halberd upon him. I treasure all the time we had together, even if..." Nadia stifled tears then, wiping them off her face with the back of her hand and clinging to Ellie.

Eoin caught on and joined in. "Aye, Ciaran does make a good fantasy hero. That brain o' his comes in handy more than once in the story, eh?"

Baltair caught the fancy as well. "Aye. Tae often I hae said Ciaran thought tae much for his ain good, being a warrior and all. I see hae that a hero needs tae use his brain as wull as his brawn."

While they yet walked toward the camp, Melina hurried out to meet Eoin, her husband. Rory followed his mother closely, visibly intent on helping to keep her safe, as befit a lad almost old enough to become a warrior.

Baltair had felt sorry for Melina when she first fell for Eoin, worried that his cousin was too stern for her. Would be gone too often. Would put her second in importance, behind his life as a time traveler. Thankfully, Baltair's fears had not come true. Melina was plainly happy as she hugged her husband and watched her son do the same.

The first indication that something was wrong was not in any of Baltair's senses. It was a vague unease that crept up his back into his hair. As a warrior, he had learned to heed these warnings.

Expecting to see a wolf, perhaps, Baltair whirled around.

A Cameron held Ellie by the mouth, silencing her as he dragged her off into the heather, kicking and flailing her arms. Nadia lay on the ground, knocked out.

Baltair's heart sank. The man might have succeeded if it weren't for that creeping unease. What had the lasses been thinking, stopping in the heather by themselves rather than staying with the rest of them?

He chided himself. The lasses hadn't known to think about their safety. They were from a time so different than this. They had no instinct to stay with the warriors. No idea how close they had to stay to be safe. This wasn't their fault. It was the warriors' fault for not protecting them.

All this went through Baltair's mind as he yelled out his war cry and rushed the Cameron.

Eoin heard and was at Baltair's side at once, even as he pushed Rory back to Melina.

The Cameron surrendered immediately when Baltair's sword reached his throat. But he didn't say a word, obstinately keeping his mouth closed.

Baltair helped Eoin bind the man's hands and gag him. "Can ye get him tae Searc withoot me?"

Eoin glanced at Ellie. "Aye. Melina?"

"Aye?"

"Ye and Rory take Nadia tae Ciaran's tent and tend her."

"Verra wull."

Baltair turned to Ellie. He couldn't leave without the lass, of course. Leaving her alone in such a vulnerable moment would be a second mistake in less than an hour's time.

Standing there blinking her eyes and not looking at anything, Ellie didn't appear to understand the danger she was in, from her inattentiveness.

Baltair reached out to her. He would offer his comfort, but he would understand if she didn't want to take it. Lasses reacted differently to being grabbed. He didn't know which way she would go.

She willingly came into his arms though, soft and smelling of lilacs.

He held her as he walked her toward camp, waiting for her to speak before he would.

She didn't say anything though, just clung to him for reassurance that she was safe.

That was fine. He gave her that reassurance.

CHAPTER THREE

I t surprised Ellie, just how quickly she recovered from being grabbed by that Cameron man. Almost immediately, she was angry, rather than afraid. Ready to fight or bite, rather than cower. Anger wasn't at all like her. She was more the pen than the sword, her usual weapon the verbal barb. But anger made her feel better than spite ever had, so she would take what she had been given and run with it.

Her finger itched again, and she twisted her new ring to scratch it.

And then she stomped on the Cameron High-lander's toe.

He didn't let go, and his grip on her was strong,

pulling her into the bushes with alarming force. No doubt more Camerons awaited him there, just like the last time one of them had grabbed her and Nadia, back in Inverness.

Rather than panic, as her old self would have done, Ellie searched her memory for a new mode of attack. Ooh, that was it. Throwing her elbow back as hard as she could, she aimed for the man's groin, but she would settle for his stomach.

He chuckled and swerved out of her reach.

Despite her new and confusing resolve to fight, she had no objections at all when Baltair and Eoin came over and fought her battle for her. She found herself thrusting with an imaginary sword when Baltair's sword swung toward the man's throat. Even more to her alarm, she was disappointed when Baltair's sword stopped short of damaging the man and only forced the man's surrender. Bloodthirst was an entirely new and foreign feeling, yet there it was.

Once the men had the situation under control and the man was being carried off for questioning, Ellie knew Baltair would come and hold her close if she feigned being upset. Baltair was like a skittish animal. You had to wait for him to come to you before you petted him, and once you were petting him, you had to do so calmly, without saying anything.

So she feigned fright.

And sure enough, he came over and opened his arms to her.

She rushed into his embrace, and it was every bit as warm and welcoming as she had imagined. She was certain he would withdraw if he knew she was clinging to him out of attraction, rather than fear. So she kept quiet, letting him lead her along.

He kept his arms around her while they followed Eoin and all the other warriors past the catapult the Murrays had built and surrounded with a wall of its ammunition of stones. Only pausing briefly to peek in and admire their handiwork, they moved on to their war chieftain Searc's tent in the center of the war camp. There were too many of them to go inside, so they all sat around Searc's campfire.

Ellie was dying to ask how they would prevent the Camerons from overhearing them. Surely there were spies out in the bushes. She thought of several wisecracks she could make about that, in order to call the proud men's attention to the problem without seeming to.

But her worries were soon allayed.

All manner of odd rhythm instruments appeared

in people's hands. Shallow handheld drums and pairs of flat sticks the people waved in their hands to make rhythmic clicking sounds. It all made enough racket that what they said would never be heard outside the circle.

Nadia must be loving this! Ellie looked for her friend but didn't see her. Oh yeah. She would be in her and Ciaran's tent. Ellie's glance went over there, but no flame of light burned inside.

Ellie still clung to Baltair, who sat the two of them down on the ground.

It was hard for Ellie, being quiet. Much of her identity was caught up in her ability to make wise-cracks and jokes. But she would keep her mouth shut as long as she could. It was Heaven, feeling Baltair's arms around her. She would just listen.

Eoin spoke. He didn't mention the book at all, but rather gave the report as if he'd been spying. "They wull attack soon." He gave an account of where the Cameron war party were camped and what they were planning.

Ellie didn't know any of it from real life, but she recognized it all from the fantasy novel. Except the catapult. That was Eoin's surprise idea from the start. He had boasted it could launch stones clear into the Cameron side of the battlefield from here.

Baltair spoke next. "They hae sent spies this way. One got verra close, and ye all hae seen him. More most like hae gotten close as wull, sae we canna count on them keeping the same position." He looked to his cousin significantly.

Eoin nodded. "Aye. 'Tis likely they wull attack from multiple sides, instead o' just one strong force as they were talking o' before. But we must needs be ready, even this night, for their attack."

The meeting went pretty much like that. Ellie didn't understand most of it, but she gathered that other scouts were being sent out. She managed to go through the whole meeting without saying one word.

Baltair's arms were still around her when everyone got up and went off to sharpen their weapons or whatever they were doing to prepare for battle. He turned to her now, deep concern in his eyes as he withdrew his arms and turned to face her on the log. "I wull hae Eoin take ye back tae yer time, where 'tis safe. Ye are na a Murray, nor a MacGregor. Ye should na hae tae face oor fate."

At one and the same time, she felt shunned and angered. He had said she didn't belong here. That she wasn't one of them. The anger made her feel stronger, so she went with that. "Nadia's not leaving, so neither am I."

He stood up and held out his hand to help her up. "That's different. Nadia is marrit tae Ciaran. Her place is by his side. But ye are neither marrit intae the clan nor born tae oor ways."

Ellie shunned the over-proud Highlander's help getting up. Instead, she turned over onto her hands and knees and held onto the log while pushing herself up.

She realized her mistake right away.

This raised her rump in the air toward him.

She felt herself blush at this, but she chose to make herself look so angry that that he would mistake her blush for anger. "I wull bide," she seethed, and then rather than stay and argue with him or let him throw her over his shoulder and carry her to Eoin, she stormed off.

For the first dozen steps, she braced herself for him to come and grab her and drag her away. What should she do in that case? Not kick and scream. That would make her look like the silly weakling he thought she was. No, she would go slack and become difficult to carry, hoping someone thought her injured and came to investigate.

But Baltair didn't come after her.

She stood for a moment, forlorn. No wonder he wasn't following. He knew she had nowhere to go.

She heard Nadia's voice. Not loud enough to make out words, but it was Nadia. She stood still and craned her head in the direction it had come from. There.

She followed Nadia's voice to her and Ciaran's tent. "Nadia, it's me, Ellie. Can I come in?"

Nadia answered right away. "Aye, ye may."

Nadia was lying against Ciaran's side, holding him close. Nadia's husband looked weak, but he was alert and aware.

"I'm sorry," Ellie said as she started to back out of the tent. "I'm intruding."

But Nadia sat up and reached out for Ellie's hand. "Nah, ye can stay. I heard a wee bit o' what Baltair said tae ye."

Grateful, Ellie smiled and took her friend's hand, letting herself be pulled inside the tent. It wasn't big.

Nadia separated out some blankets from her and Ciaran's bedding. "Here, now ye hae yer ain pallet. Gae on and lie doon."

Ellie was on the verge of imitating an inch worm as she wriggled into place, in order to get some laughs, but one look at Ciaran's sickly face made her think better of that idea. So she just lay down and examined the roof of the plaid woolen tent. "Thanks be tae the both o' ye. I did na want tae gae back tae

Baltair, but I would na hae had any choice, if ye had na hae let me in."

Nadia took her hand and gave it a friendly and quite reassuring squeeze. "He did na mean it that way, ye ken. He just does na want ye tae be hurt."

What her friend said made sense, of course, but Ellie fought tears until she lost the battle. First one fell down her cheek, then another. "I was just starting tae feel like a member o' a clan, with ye and Ciaran, and Eoin and Baltair. Certies, we dinna always get along. But we plan like kin, it seemed tae me. Did I imagine it?"

Nadia jiggled their joined hands. "Nay, ye didna imagine it. Ye are part o' the clan. Baltair would na care sae much what befell ye, if ye were na. He is ainly thinking o' the battle that comes, and what the best way would be tae keep ye safe."

Ciaran's voice came from the other side of Nadia. "Sing us a song, my love. Give us a fair vision o' hope tae send us off tae a fine dreamland."

"Aye," Ellie agreed. "Please, Nadia."

Nadia sang to her and Ciaran a silly song, and gradually, Ellie relaxed and went to sleep.

There was a knight, in a summer's night,

Was riding ower the lee, diddle.

And there he saw a bonny birdy,

Was singing upon a tree, diddle.
O wow for day, diddle.
And dear gin, it were day, diddle.
Gin it were day, an gin I were away!
For I ha na lang time to stay, diddle...

CHAPTER FOUR

With a wry smile on his face, Baltair watched Ellie go. As soon as she realized she was in unfamiliar territory surrounded by people she didn't know well, she would come back to him.

But then she heard something he didn't and went in search of it, culminating in Nadia at the tent door, letting Ellie in.

Connell's voice came from behind him. "I ken ye want tae grab her and carry her haime, then leave her there, sae why dinna ye?"

Baltair sighed as he turned to Eoin's second-oldest brother. "On the morrow wull be soon enough. I wull na disturb Ciaran. Oor cousin has it rough enough. Ye ken the druids crippled him?"

Connell nodded. "Aye, that I dae."

Baltair headed off toward Searc and beckoned Connell to follow him, which his cousin did.

Searc at first opened up his arms, but then his face changed and he realized it wasn't Meehall, probably because of something in Baltair's face. "The two o' ye are wide awake, I see. Wull then, take first watch. Northeast." He gestured with his thumb over his shoulder and watched the two of them leave that way.

"This is Meehall's twin," Baltair told anyone who started to greet Connell. He knew the news would spread, so he didn't worry about making an announcement.

The two of them made their way to the trees on the periphery of the camp's forest, then began their three-hour watch for Cameron spies in the moonlit heather beyond. Speaking in whispers throughout, they kept the conversation on family. Baltair learned a great deal from Connell.

Tavish and Kelsey were still at Dunskey castle, of course, with Kelsey stopping in at Druidville — Eoin's nickname for Celtic University— as often as she pleased, thanks to a teleportation ring. Other family members also thought Kelsey had become too much of a druid now and was sadly not as trustworthy. At one time, she had been their shining example. Now, she was the black sheep of the MacGregor family.

Tomas and Amber were down in Australia half the year and back in the future United States the other half of the year, helping run the Renaissance faire. Dall and Ellie had negotiated better time travel for the family, and also more control over the faire. Tomas wanted everyone else to come help with the faire, so that the whole family could be together.

Meehall and Sarah were at Murray castle, helping the Murray in his attempt to keep Scotland from uniting with England. The Scottish parliament seemed intent on accepting England's offer, but the Scottish people didn't want it. The Murray was one of the few leaders who honored his clan's opinions. The lasses had warned him that Scotland would enter into a union with England in 1707, but Baltair held out hope The Murray would prevent it. This battle with the Camerons would distract his efforts, if the Camerons prevailed and claimed his lands.

Connell had let Ashley go when they all found out about their curse to serve the druids. Unlike Tavish, Tomas, and Meehall, he hadn't reunited with Ashley. That was all he would say in the matter, and so Baltair let him go on to the next sibling in the bunch.

Eoin's twin, who had been Christened Jeffrey but had chosen the more Scottish name Friseal for himself, still wandered the world, in search of his purpose in life. He had dumped Lauren, his faire girlfriend, mere weeks before their wedding. She had become an engineer, then settled at Inverurie in the time of the Battle of Harlaw. She was happily married to the local Laird, and her friend was happily married to the laird's brother.

Baltair told Connell that Eoin had let his faire girlfriend go. Jaelle was in the time of Hadrian's Wall, happily married to a Celtic Pict and full of tales of magic woad decorations, whenever they heard from her.

Their two faces were animated from talking about their MacGregor clan, so it was disconcerting when Connell looked Baltair in the eye and spoke seriously. "'Tis wrong o' ye tae decide Ellie's fate, ye ken. If ye are sae fashit aboot her safety, then mayhap ye should teach her tae fight."

Baltair picked up a rock and threw it out into the heather, laughing when a Cameron spy yelled out in objection. "I feel responsible for the lass. I dinna ken what I would dae if ill befell her."

Connell picked up a rock and aimed at the same place where Baltair had thrown his, but the Cameron men must've moved, because there wasn't any yell this time. "Ye canna stop her from turning aroond and coming right back—"

"I wull tell Eoin nay tae bring her back—"

"Then she wull gae tae Kelsey. Is that what ye want?"

Baltair turned from trying to find the Cameron men. "Why would she gae tae Kelsey? Ellie works at Celtic. She kens the meaning o' Kelsey's druid robes."

Connell's head dipped in an attitude that said he couldn't believe what he was hearing. He waited there as if what Baltair had said was a joke. When Baltair didn't say anything, he gave an incredulous smile. "Ellie fancies ye. She wull na be easy tae keep away."

Baltair shook his head and picked up another rock, finding it easier to look out at the heather than into the certainty in Connell's eyes. "She does na fancy me. She imagines life in this time is like that fantasy novel we read." The more he spoke, the slower the words came, because he knew even as he said them that they were not true.

Connell pointed to a bush that had just moved, then bent to pick up another rock.

* * *

Baltair scooped up two mugs of breakfast mash and headed over to Ciaran's tent to wait for Ellie to come out. When she did, he handed her one and walked her over to the nearest campfire, making a place for her to sit down as he sat next to her. "If ye are gaun'ae stay with us here," he looked around at all the other Murrays sitting nearby who could hear them and left it at that, without adding 'in my time.'"Then ye wull need tae ken how tae defend yerself. 'Twill na be easy. It falls upon me tae teach ye, sae eat up and get ready for yer lesson."

At the mention of the fact that he would be teaching her, Ellie's face lit up in a way that he couldn't deny she did fancy him.

As soon as she had eaten the last bite and set her mug down in the pile, he took her hand and tugged her over to the practice area in the camp.

She moved as if to join the other men practicing with each other, silly lass that she was.

Baltair looked where the children were practicing, but he knew that would raise her ire and be counterproductive, so he grabbed a few practice swords, handed her one, and took her over to an unused corner of the practice area, just the two of them. "First, ye need tae ken how tae walk with yer sword..." He showed her all the attacks and all the parries, running through them quickly and making her mimic each one until she had them all.

"Wull I be ready for when the battle comes?" she asked between moves.

"Nay," he barked out. "And ye wull na gae near the battle."

She scowled, and she looked adorable.

He ruthlessly threw her into heavy practice, determined to make her see she just was not strong enough for sword battle. Or, to make her stronger.

"Coome at me," he said to her with a careful look on his face, not encouraging and not discouraging either. It was the face he always used when sparring with a beginner. The fact that these people were usually six years old rather than fully grown lasses with distracting endowments was beside the matter.

Ellie smiled wide as she raised the practice sword up and ran at him, preparing to hit him with all she was worth.

He easily parried her hit, and he did it harder than he needed to. In very slow and exaggerated moves, he raised his own sword and began his own attack, giving her the time she needed to respond, but only barely. When she was ready, he came at her, still in slow motion but willing her to mess up the parry so that he would have an excuse to get Eoin and take her back to her time.

But she made it. She hit his blunted wooden practice sword away from her just in time to avoid injury, had it been a true weapon.

He kept at this, ruthlessly making her go through the movements she just learned, deliberately trying to exhaust her. He knew he wasn't being merciful, but would the enemy be merciful? No.

They spent the better half of the day in relentless practice, until Ellie was nearly falling down every time she went to block a blow. Blisters were forming on her hands, and her face was an unholy shade of red.

What had he done?

"Aye," he said, putting his practice sword away in the bin. "That's enough for now. We gae back tae Ciaran's tent sae I can tend tae yer blisters."

"Nay," she huffed out through deep breaths. I dinna want tae be babied. I'm strong enough tae handle this. Let's keep gang. Everyone else is still practicing, sae I should be, as wull."

Without giving it another thought, Baltair scooped Ellie up and carried her to Ciaran and Nadia's tent. Only when he stood outside it did a moment of hesitation come. "Ciaran, Ellie took wull tae the sparring, and she is blistered. I dinna ken where else tae bring her. Tongues would wag if I took her tae my ain tent. Can I bring her inside and tend tae her wounds?"

Within the tent, Ciaran said to Nadia, "Let them in."

Baltair thought he heard something in the distance as well, but the scouts would see to that.

Nadia's voice was the one that came out to Baltair. "O' course. Coome in. Here, I wull open the flap." Her face was impressed when she looked at Baltair holding Ellie. And a bit gloating.

He couldn't let Nadia or Ellie entertain the wrong idea. He gruffly carried Ellie in and laid her down on the pallet where she'd slept the night before, judging by how Nadia and Ciaran were sitting on the other pallet together. "Let's see what manner o' salve ye hae in those famous satchels o' yers," he said to Nadia while he took Ellie's boots off. He expected Ellie to fight him, but she was oddly silent. Submissive, even. That was the last thing he expected from the fiery redhead.

Nadia grabbed her bag and rummaged inside. "Och, aye. We hae some great stuff. Here." She handed him a tiny tin.

He opened it to find tiny paper packets. For just a moment, he marveled at them, again dismissing distant sounds that tugged at his attention, but that he dismissed as someone else's immediate concern.

Because Nadia was whispering, "Ye open them tae reveal the Band-Aids inside. They are sticky around the cushion meant for the blister. Ye stick them on her feet, ye ken, sae that the blister canna pop."

Baltair inspected Ellie's feet. Just as he had suspected, they were blistered as well as her hands. She wasn't accustomed to being on her feet so much. He'd never seen such big blisters forming, and it made him feel bad. With a heavy sigh, he turned to the Band-Aids.

Smiling, Nadia opened the first one and put it on the first blister, showing him.

With a sense of awe, Baltair put Band-Aids on the rest of Ellie's blisters, both on her hands and on her feet, then put her socks and boots back on.

When Ellie spoke up, it was to call attention to something Baltair had been dismissing. "Whate'er be the din that comes? It sounds like a parade."

Baltair tsked and was about to dismiss her musings when Ciaran put a hand on his arm and held up his other hand for silence.

This time, Baltair truly listened. Sure enough, another war party approached. From the tones on their small pipes, they were friendly. But in the Highlands, you never could be too sure.

CHAPTER FIVE

N ow that attention had been called to the blisters on her feet, it was painful for Ellie to walk. Thankfully, Baltair had put on enough Band-Aids. They would allow her feet to heal properly.

It'd been difficult to sit still and let him minister to her. However, her new sixth sense told her it was the only way she would have him near her. If she looked too ready to handle it herself, he would storm off, impatient with her as usual for not being ready to deal with things in his time.

He helped her get up, and Nadia helped Ciaran up, and the four of them left the tent together, the couples arm-in-arm.

Nadia and Ellie gasped at the same time. Who did they see at the head of this new war party, leading dozens and dozens of kilted highlanders, and all dolled up in a kilt himself? None other than the author of that fantasy book about Ciaran, Harold Cochran. This was the younger version, though. Gone was the gray hair. In its place was a fiery red mane that resembled Ellie's own head of hair.

Ellie looked Harold straight in the eye and waited for him to approach her. She needed to find out if this younger version of the famous author knew about time travel. She would whisper to him when he came over. What should she say, 'How lang hae ye been here?' Yes, that would do the trick.

But Harold's attention was held by the approach of the Murray clan war party's chief, Searc.

Flanked by several highlanders in Murray plaid, Searc was approaching slow and stately, with his kilt swinging in the wind. "Ràild MacEacharna. Never thought tae see the likes o' ye here in Murray lands and na in oor castle. Why hae ye ventured sae far?"

All the Murray warriors nodded in agreement and interest. Stopping at parade rest, feet slightly apart, they made an attentive audience to the spectacle of an unexpected ally.

Harold addressed Searc stoically. "What does it matter, why I hae coome? Here I am, offering the aid o' the MacEacharnas. Wull ye accept, or wull we walk on by? "Tis nay matter tae us, but it could be o' great significance tae ye, I am thinking." He caught Ellie's eye then and winked as if he had told a great joke.

She smiled at him openly in response. It was automatic. But then she remembered she was trying to see if he was a time traveler or not. With this in mind, she quickly racked her brain for something she could do that only someone from the future would recognize. Inspired, she made the OK sign with her right hand and raised it up toward Harold, searching the man's face for a knowing look that would tell her he knew she was from the 21st century.

Either he wasn't yet a time traveler, or he feared giving her away as one, because he didn't respond.

Searc, on the other hand, didn't hesitate to respond to Harold. "We dae accept yer help. We accept it with open arms." He held his arms open where he stood, surrounded by his Murray warriors.

Harold stepped up and ceremoniously walked into Searc's arms, where the two clasped both fore-arms and shook, then heartily slapped each other on the back, which was greeted by cheers from both men's warriors.

Searc took charge of the group once more. "Coome, let us plan how yer aid wull best be used."

He turned and led everyone toward his campfire, where they had spoken the night before.

Baltair helped Ciaran, and the two rushed after the other warriors, joining up with Eoin and Connell.

Ellie turned to follow them. Now certain this was a young and non-time-traveling Harold, she needed to know what their plans would be. She would subtly add to their discussion of battle plans the insights she had gleaned from reading future Harold's book about this very battle that was about to take place in a few days. Sure, Baltair, Ciaran, and Eoin had read it too, but women noticed different things than the men would.

Nadia grabbed Ellie's arm and held her there.

Ellie turned to her friend with annoyance. "Whatever ye hae tae say can wait!"

Nadia shook her head no, leaning in as if to whisper.

Watching the men go out of earshot and throwing her hand up in exasperation, Ellie leaned over to let Nadia whisper whatever this was going to be.

Nadia's whisper was calm and cool in Ellie's ear. "There is na point in cooming up with a plan tae win the battle while the Camerons hae that druid child

Tahra on their side, strengthened by the magic halberd."

All the blood drained from Ellie's face, and she leaned on her friend for support. How had she forgotten about the halberd, the very thing that had crippled Ciaran? A heavy weight fell upon the mood, and Ellie looked at Nadia now in despair, with tears in her eyes.

Nadia pulled Ellie back into the tent, whispering, "It will na dae tae hae folk see us doubting. The more confident the warriors are, the better."

Ellie nodded as the two of them sat down, side-by-side in the tent. "Did ye get the feeling the Camerons would hae been fine withoot Tahra aboot?"

Nadia grabbed her hand and squeezed, then held it while whispering, "Aye, especially Fergus. He cow-towed when she was aboot, but then when she would gae off intae the woods, he started tae be nice again. If Meehall had na rescued as, I was gaun'ae ask Fergus tae let us gae."

Ellie squeezed Nadia's hand back. "As was I. Or Gille."

"Aye, Gille was nice as wull. He was the one who gave us a little ale in the stead o' water that time, remember?"

"Aye, and Dougal always saw tae it we had blankets at night."

Nadia opened her arms wide. "'Twas na just the three of them, either. Nearly all o' them had sympathetic eyes when Tahra was na near."

"She kens it, tae. Betimes, I did think she was gaun'ae order them aught, and then she changed her mind, thinking better o' it."

"Certies, I was, that she would hae us whipped, when we sat crying and na doing her bidding, when we first arrived in the Cameron war camp."

Ellie nodded. "Wull I ken."

Nadia went on. "But there was some aught in the set of the men's jaws. In their posture."

Ellie grabbed Nadia's hand anew. "Aye. I remember thinking, "Gae ahead, ye witch. Order these strong highlanders tae dae things against their common decency. And then we shall see.""

Nadia's whisper got faster. "Oor minds they were as one, then. Spent my time daydreaming what would happen if Tahra stepped ower the line and went tae far. My favorite fantasy was when they tied her arms and legs to four different horses and telt the horses tae run in opposing ways, pulling her asunder."

Disgusting is this idea was, it had a certain

appeal to Ellie. She had felt so helpless as the Camerons captive, so put upon. Ellie laughed —and immediately put her hand over her mouth and listened in case anyone had heard. The last thing they needed was somebody coming close and listening in.

When Ellie heard nothing, she went on. "Drawing and quartering, they call that. I did na think o' them dang that tae the druid child, but I sure wanted her hung upside doon from a tree by her ankles, sae that all the blood rushed tae her head."

Nadia nodded and squeezed Ellie's hand again. "Aye, we were given all the worst food tae eat and naught but water tae drink —and scarcely enough o' that."

Ellie slumped against her friend. "How could I hae forgotten Tahra was still here with the Camerons?"

Nadia raised her eyebrows at Ellie and opened her eyes significantly.

Ellie shrugged. "What?"

With the ghost of a smile, Nadia whispered, "Ye hae been distracted by Baltair."

Ellie grimaced an apology. "Wull I am nay longer gaun'ae be. We need tae get that halberd away from Tahra. The men are all concentrating on battle.

Methinks them tae proud tae admit the halberd is tae much for them tae beat."

Nadia held up her hands as if to stop a team of horses. "Hauld on, now. I dinna think two lasses are gaun'ae get that halberd. Howsoever, mayhap we can find oot exactly where it is and tell Ciaran and Baltair."

Ellie smiled at Nadia, grateful to have a friend here in this beautiful but oh-so-difficult time. "Aye, let us gae find oot. The scouts are sure tae hae heard aboot it."

Nadia got up, pulling Ellie up too, then leaning in to whisper, "We need errands tae be aboot, in the camp."

Ellie gestured out the tent door. "Mayhap we should find some other lasses and join in with them till we ken oor way?"

Nadia shrugged into Ellie with her shoulder affectionately. "Ye hae tae much sense."

Ellie held her breath while Nadia pulled back the tent flap, nervous lest there be someone out there listening after all. But there wasn't, and the two of them rushed out, exchanged a glance, and walked among the tents.

Except for the scouts and those guarding the camp, the Murray men were still around the campfire, beating drums to hide the sounds of their planning. From the look of it, they would be for quite some time.

At long last, Ellie and Nadia wandered to where they saw Murray women walking with buckets and followed them to the stream. Six Murray men stood guard, two with bows and the rest with swords.

Nadia met Ellie's gaze and raised her eyebrows.

Ellie shrugged and walked down toward the stream, getting in line to carry a bucket of water back up to the camp and noticing Nadia right behind her.

No one was talking, and that wasn't helpful.

Ellie's pesky finger itched again, and she turned the ring around, having to do so three times to stop the infernal itch.

She needed to speak to the nearest guard. "Has that druid child made an appearance yet, the one with the magic halberd which crippled Nadia's husband?"

At first, the guard had a surprised, 'now that you mention it' look about him, but he shrugged it off quickly. "Aye, Tahra joined the Cameron camp in the wee hours this morrow."

Confident with this information, Ellie and Nadia dumped their water in the nearest stew pot and went back to their tent. Once they were seated inside,

Ellie resolved to come up with a plan to fix the situation.

Her finger itched again, and she twisted the ring.

Nadia looked at Ellie's ring with concern on her face for a moment.

Ellie made a funny face at her. "We wull sneak in and steal the halberd while Tahra's asleep. We wull destroy it with fire. Mayhap that will break Ciaran's crippling curse."

CHAPTER SIX

L ate into the night around the fire, Baltair and the other men tried to plan an effective strategy with Ràild MacEacharna.

Eoin was more vocal than everyone else, as usual. "A tried-and-true strategy is tae attack them with a heavy force from one side and push them toward the cliffs. I dinna see why that canna work."

It was the exact strategy used in the fantasy book, of course. Baltair couldn't believe how obtuse Eoin was being. Eoin knew Tahra was there and had read the book.

Ràild raised his palm up in a sign of hopeless-ness. "That might hae worked when they did na ken we were here, but 'tis clear they ken, by the spy ye hae captured, if na by all the noise in the heather. Surprise will na work, this time."

Eoin looked at the man with exasperation. "We hae the catapult, ye ken. We can attack from a great distance. 'Tis na at all the same."

Baltair raised his voice before Eoin said something that shouldn't be overheard by the others. "He has the right o' it, Eoin. The enemy is aware o' us. They hae been spying. We hae tae ditch the auld plan and coome up with some aught new."

Ràild's men were not quite integrated into the Murray warriors. They had gathered around the circle all right, but they were bunched up on one side, while the Murray men were bunched up on the other. The opposition that this symbolized was not lost on Baltair. Neither was it lost on either side of men. They were all sizing each other up, and now that the talking had begun, there were boasts.

One of Ràild's men said, "It should na take as long to win this battle for you. The last battle we won only took an afternoon."

Baltair was ready to give the man a piece of his mind.

But Ràild stepped in and did it himself. "Quiet with ye. Each battle is different, and I hae a feeling this one wull be an epic battle, lasting days rather than hoors. The terrain is tricky, ye ken. The plan was tae run the Camerons off the cliff, but the Camerons hae caught waard o' that. Sae it will na be sae simple, nor sae quick. In any case, nay battle was e'er won with boasting." He cast his glance over at Ciaran's lame leg and lingered for a long moment with a grimace.

Eoin noticed and stepped forward, looking straight at Ràild. "Tis true we wull hae tae dae without Ciaran for this battle, but I did na enter the clan till recently. Mayhap they dinna ken my ain prowess. Mayhap that wull help us win the victory."

Raild shook his head no. "E'en I hae heard tell o' ye, Eoin, way far away in MacEacharna lands. Ye hae been here two years, aye?"

Instead of answering the question, Eoin fired off another of his own. "Wull, we hae kept the catapult a secret, aye?"

Eoin was nothing if not aggressive. Always seeking out battle rather than a way to avoid battle. The truth of the matter was Eoin fought for glory. Ciaran, on the other hand, had always fought for the good of the clan.

Baltair needed to leave this scene before he said something he would regret or actually started a fight with his younger but much bigger and more bull-headed cousin.

He backed away, then rounded the backs of the men until he found Searc. "I wish tae gae up the mountain and view the enemy camp for ideas."

Searc looked over at Eoin, then back at Baltair, then winked and gave Baltair his torque, to wear for passage out of the camp.

Baltair showed the torque to the sentries and rode up the mountain, taking out his disgust with the men on the difficult terrain, which the horse easily trampled. The Murrays were out of ideas and out of options. They needed to welcome these helpers in with open arms, not quibble with them. They needed to be a united force, not a bunch of men striving after individual glory and acclaim.

The moonlight on the rocks made for an easy trip up the mountain, and he kept going until he had a good view of both camps, Murray and Cameron.

He froze when he heard another horse coming up behind him, then rode behind a large rock, dismounted, and crawled out the other way on his elbows through the bushes, dirk in hand.

Crouching in the darkness, he wondered as usual when awaiting a fight if this would be his last. If he would lose. He had been stupid to ride up here by himself. What had he been thinking? Maybe it would only be one man, and he would be able to hold his own. The trail was pretty narrow. If he crawled forward a bit, he could cut the horse's ankles from the side and make the rider fall.

He inched along in the dark earthy place beneath the brush on the side of the hill below the faint trail he'd followed. He'd been here once before, with Eoin and Ciaran.

* * *

THE THREE OF THEM RODE SINGLE FILE, IDLY talking as usual, making their way over this mountain to spy on the Camerons, who at the time were farther north. It was one of the rare occasions when Eoin talked of the larger MacGregor clan, how angry it made him to have the name expunged from the records and made illegal to use, all because of the Campbells' arrogance.

Eoin flexed and strengthened his muscles by lifting rocks while he rode —which he also did while he ate and while he did just about everything, God bless his wife. Eoin always assumed leadership when they ventured away from the Murrays. After all, he had the object that allowed time travel.

But Ciaran had always been the most loyal of them. The one who had his back, Baltair knew.

Baltair was at the back of the group of three, with his back unguarded this time. And it wasn't the Camerons who attacked this time, but the weather.

A typical Highlands storm had come up just as they reached these heights, dumping an uncommon amount of water on the dirt trail and making it slick. The horses became even more skittish than normal warhorses are, blowing great puffs of air out of their nostrils and slapping their tails back and forth, stomping their feet.

"We canna stay here on the trail," Baltair said to his cousins.

"'Tis verra steep," Eoin agreed, bellowing over the wind and rain. "Let us keep gang up till we reach the shelter o' the rocks on the other side. 'Tis na far, and we wull gae slow."

Both of them looked to Ciaran to make the tie-breaking decision. Their mutual cousin sat there between them longer than either expected him to, thinking it over. When at last he spoke, it was against the grain.

"I think we should stay here," Ciaran said, surprising them both. "'Tis na safe tae move, and na likely we wull catch oor death o' cauld. We are Highlanders, accustomed tae the cauld. Bundle up in yer plaid."

It was true. The wool these plaid blankets were made of did keep one warm even when wet. It was why all the clans had traded a few cows in for sheep. Just a few. Enough to provide wool for the clan, and no more.

"Ye hae the right o' it," Baltair told Ciaran. "Ye hae more sense than the two o' us." Her gave Ciaran a small smile and a nod, getting his plaid ready to wrap around his shoulders and over his head to keep them warm through the storm and reining his horse in to keep the steed steady, which pleased the horse much more than moving had, after all.

But Eoin had not agreed. No, their hot-headed cousin was not happy to be sitting through the storm wrapped in wet wool and shivering. "Nay, we wull ride up as I said. Yah!" And with that, Eoin not only rode up himself, but reached back and slapped Ciaran's horse so that it too started up the hill.

Herd animals that they are, horses are more likely to follow each other than not. This is what happened with Baltair's horse. Even though Baltair had reined him in and steadied him, he started to move up the hill after the other two. Baltair had taken his hands off the reins and loosened his legs in order to pull half of his plaid up around himself and be warm. Baltair fell.

And then Ciaran proved his loyalty, love, and an uncanny talent with horses. Baltair's younger cousin was able to steady his own horse, get down, catch Baltair before he fell down the hill, grab Baltair's horse, and calm it. It all happened in a few seconds. Ciaran didn't even break a sweat. Of course, he did have rain pouring over him.

Ciaran held onto Baltair's wrist and pulled him back up the hill from where he'd fallen, then paused and looked Baltair up and down from head to toe, not stopping until he was satisfied there was no blood. "Does it hurt tae move anything?"

"Nay," Baltair assured him. "I thank ye for saving me." Baltair looked down the hill. Not far down at all, it broke off into a steep cliff that fell a hundred times the height of a man. "I owe ye my life," Baltair told Ciaran. "I wull repay ye, if ever ye ask."

Ciaran hugged him then. A manly hug between cousins, full of fists pounding on backs. But a hug, nonetheless. "It wull ne'er coome tae that. I would lay down my life for any o' my clan, and I ken ye would dae the same. Any o' us would."

But both of them knew that last part wasn't true.

Because Eoin hadn't even stopped. He was nowhere to be seen.

* * *

AT LONG LAST, THE RIDER BECAME VISIBLE under the moonlight, rounding the mountain trail a dozen steps below Baltair's position.

Baltair let out a deep breath, took in another, and let it out again, relaxing.

The rider was Ràild. Ostensibly, the man was a warrior in his prime. But Baltair had seen a portrait of the man with grey hair, on the back of the book, so he was watching the man much more closely than he watched other allies. Raild sat his horse like an old man, not like the young man he was outwardly. This was not the young Raild. It was the older Raild, come back to relive this battle in his past. Why?

Baltair didn't greet the man, just crawled backward until he was out of the brush and stood, so he could be seen. He didn't go into the path where the horse might trample him. He didn't know Ràild well, after all.

Ràild raised a hand in greeting, dismounted, and led the horse up to Baltair while he spoke. "Ye are Ellie's man, aye?"

Baltair flinched.

Ràild's brow wrinkled. "Certies I did see ye arm-in-arm with Ellie?"

There wasn't any point in arguing with the man, so Baltair nodded.

Ràild gave him a knowing look and might even have winked as he patted his horse's neck. "I ken ye disagree with the antics o' my men and how I dinna stop them. But ye hae na seen some o' the horrors I hae seen. I strive tae prepare my men as best I can."

Baltair took out a piece of paper and a pencil that Nadia had given him out of her notebook for such a time as this.

Ràild's eyes opened wide at the sight, and he looked at Baltair with new meaning, his face saying as clear as if he had said, "Och! Ye are from the future as wull!"

Baltair shook his head to deny being from the future as he scrawled a note to Ràild. "Nay, I am na from the future, though I hae visited there. Howsoever, I dae ken the horrors ye hae seen. I read yer book, the one aboot my cousin Ciaran and the coming battle—"

Ràild's face lit up with the delight that comes from being understood, and he clapped Baltair on the back. "Och, even better! I—"

Baltair gently covered the man's mouth. "Nah aloud."

Ràild's brow wrinkled again, but he stopped talking.

Baltair let the man see the relief on his face, then resumed writing. "Hae ye aught upon ye that the druids gave ye for time travel? We think the druids can listen tae oor talk through these items, sae we hae taken tae writing instead o' speaking—"

Ràild grabbed the paper, shaking his head violently, and scrawled his own message. "The druid child Tahra also read my book, sae the rules o' battle hae completely changed! Dinna ye see? We hae na telling what may pass. I dinna ken how we are tae prevail unless we ask the faeries for help."

Too impatient to spend the time writing, Baltair briefly considered and then said, "Ye did ask the faeries for help. 'Tis in the book."

Ràild's face grew pained. "That was an embell-ishment."

Baltair's anger took hold of him, and he raised his voice at the man, resisting the urge to push him. "An embellishment? Here we are depending on yer book for oor strategy in this battle, and the most important part is an embellishment?"

Ràild moved to put his hand on Baltair's arm.

Baltair moved his arm, but he stopped and listened.

Ràild nodded to acknowledge the favor. "I didna tell ye tae depend upon my book. If I kenned that was what the lasses were aboot when they asked for it, I ne'er would hae telt them o' it. 'Tis why I came back, tae make it right."

Baltair whirled toward his horse. He had to go warn his cousins.

This time, Ràild did lay a hand on Baltair's arm. It felt oddly steady, making him pause and turn to the man. But this would be Ràild's last chance to speak to him before Baltair told the others he was full of something ruder than beans.

The older man looked deep into Baltair's eyes, plainly willing him to put doubt aside and hear him out. "But it could be possible, ye ken. Tae bargain with the faeries for an item such as that. 'Twould require a sacrifice—"

Baltair cursed. "A sacrifice! Ye are na better than that evil druid child Tahra!"

Something caught his eye, down between the trees at the bottom of the mountain.

Baltair broke his gaze away from trying to cow Ràild.

There. Right there in the brush was movement.

It was only discernible because the moonlight reflected off the thistles amid the brush between the sparse trees in the valley on this side of the mountain. Two figures moved from the Murray camp toward the Cameron camp. Two figures unaccustomed to walking amid Scottish thistles.

Baltair was already getting on his horse and urging it back down the mountain. "The lasses! We must stop them!"

He didn't expect Ràild to follow him, but he was glad when the older man did.

CHAPTER SEVEN

E llie's right ring finger itched as if it had been bitten by ten mosquitoes at the same time. Over and over again, she kept turning her ring to scratch the itch. It worked, but only until she started to relax again into creeping toward Cameron camp. As soon as she dared to feel relieved and start to relax and have doubts she was doing the right thing, the itch came back. She pulled the ring toward her fingertip a little, to see if it was making a mark. Nope. Weird. Oh well. No harm in wearing it, then.

The sounds of horses blowing and stamping ahead in the dark told her they were nearly at Cameron camp. It was time to tell Nadia just enough of the plan that she would be able to help. Just in case.

The Highland sky was clear of clouds for once, and the moon shone brightly on the tall grass and trees. Ellie ducked into the shadow behind a boulder and put her back to it so that no Camerons could take her by surprise, then waited for Nadia.

Her friend arrived without a sound, startling her.

Ellie put her hand to her heart, showing her surprise.

Nadia grinned an apology.

Ellie got her pepper spray out of her PenUlt Survival backpack. Nudging Nadia, she showed it to her, whispering, "Get this oot, and be ready tae use it."

Nadia's look said, "'Tis in jest, ye are."

A sudden renewal of her itch made Ellie groan with impatience as she rubbed it. Still, she kept her voice down. "Ye hae used pepper spray afore, aye?"

Nadia shook her head no.

Ellie groaned some more, now in frustration.

With a betrayed look in her eyes, Nadia raised her hands up, whispering, "I hae heard o' pepper spray. I ken what it does. I just hae na e'er used it. Is all right with ye?" She pointed at Ellie's hands. "Mayhap ye should take that ring off."

The battle against the Camerons loomed over their heads, and Nadia was worried about a ring?

Ellie threw her hands out in a dismissive gesture, hissing, "O' course all is right with me. 'Tis ainly that I (She put a strong emphasis on the word 'I' while wrinkling her brow at her friend.) am fierce intae oor mission." Ellie took a deep fortifying breath, reminding herself that Nadia was friend, not enemy, then whispered, "'Tis easy. Just get as close tae the eyes as ye can and spray it. Here, try. Pretend like this tree is a Cameron guard. This knot is his eye."

Nadia was a graceful dancer. Unlike Ellie, her feet didn't make any noise. It was eerie how quiet she was, walking over to the tree. "Why the sudden need for me tae use pepper spray?" Nadia whispered over her shoulder. But without waiting for an answer, she pointed the can at the tree and sprayed the knot.

Ellie raised her fists in the air as if she were cheering for a football team, then beckoned Nadia back into the shadow of the boulder and whispered. "Good. That be it. Ye got close enough. 'Tis important tae get close enough. Otherwise, 'twill sting, but 'twill na stop the attacker."

Nadia put her hands on her hips and swayed in that way she had when she wanted you to get to the point. "Ye hae na answered my question," she whispered. "Why the need for me tae ken how tae use pepper spray?"

Ellie leaned over and barely whispered in Nadia's ear, "We wull hae tae take doon at least one guard in order tae enter the camp, is why."

Ugh, her infernal finger was itching again.

Ellie turned the ring.

Blissfully, the itching stopped.

Nadia had turned white. "I agreed tae coome spy with ye. Tae find oot where Tahra is sleeping. I did na agree tae take oot any guards. What in the waurld are ye thinking?"

With an impatient sigh, Ellie leaned in and whispered to Nadia at length, explaining what she had in mind.

* * *

Ellie had finally caught sight of the most likely guard to take out. He was by himself, his partner having run over to the next pair of guards. "Now is oor chance, Nadia. I hae tae gae now."

Nadia looked like she might be sick, but with eyes as wide as saucers, she had agreed to the plan.

Ellie gestured for Nadia to crawl, so the guard wouldn't see her.

Nadia complied, tying the hem of her long dress up around her waist to make this possible. Her woolen stockings and linen bloomers would be adequate protection from the prickly dry grass.

The guard didn't have a bow, only a sword and shield, so he couldn't get her from a distance. It was another reason Ellie had chosen this guard.

This was it.

Ellie loosened the bodice of her dress at the top, then stepped out into the path in site of the guard, arms up.

He saw her immediately, and he took a stance with his sword out, relaxing only slightly when he saw that she was female and unarmed.

Ellie's finger itched unbearably now.

Not taking the time to scratch it, she stuck her chest out and swayed sensuously in the way she'd seen sirens do in the movies.

The guard looked toward where his fellow guard had gone.

Ellie used the opportunity to make sure Nadia was ready, pepper spray in hand.

Nadia was. Good.

Finally, he came to her. "'Twill na last long. I fear yer ain pleasure wull na be satisfied. But I canna say nay."

She raised her chest toward his face.

He was so strong and large and heavy that he

probably figured she didn't stand a chance. He moved in, with his face to her chest.

Ellie ducked her head aside while Nadia reached around and sprayed his face with the pepper spray and handed Ellie the handcuffs.

Click, click went the handcuffs as Ellie joined his wrists together. Then she clipped his ankles together as well.

Meanwhile, Nadia gagged him.

Ellie clipped his wrists to his ankles.

Together, they pushed him over and rolled him into the bushes, where hopefully it would take a while for him to be found. The last thing they did was tie his ankles together so he couldn't get up or walk.

Ellie grabbed the poor man's plaid off of his body and wrapped herself in it. Now she looked like a Cameron woman, outside to relieve herself and chilled by the night air. Headed back to her tent. At a run.

* * *

Tahra's tent was easy to spot in the camp, being the one most heavily guarded. Ellie's mind was full of imaginary things she was saying to Nadia.

Don't forget your next part, Nadia. Please remember.

Just when Ellie had to either pass by Tahra's tent or look like she was up to something suspicious, she heard in the distance the angry cries of the guard they had tied up and gagged. "Ye let me gae, ye wee strumpet!" It was loud enough to be heard from here, but not so loud that it would wake anyone.

Tahra's tent guards turned to see what all the commotion was about.

This was Ellie's chance, and she took it, sneaking into the tent.

Tahra lay asleep, looking more like a child than a druid, beautiful and innocent. Such an illusion. She had plainly been clutching the halberd when she went to bed, but now it lay alone beside her.

Ellie reached out toward the halberd after moving around to the foot of Tahra's pallet. She would grab the halberd, duck under the side of the tent away from the guards, and run. So close. So close to being able to destroy it. Hopefully this would uncripple Nadia's husband and give the Murrays a fair chance at winning the battle foretold in Cochran's book.

Two things happened the instant Ellie touched the halberd:

One, the halberd spoke to her. "Hello, Dearie. I can give ye power. Power beyond yer wildest dreams." It showed her.

In her imagination, Ellie held the halberd high at the scene of the battle. Baltair, Ciaran, Eoin, Connell, and all of their Murray warrior friends were behind her. Good men, ready to fight for the lands their cattle had roamed for generations.

But they only had swords and bows to fight with.

In the halberd's vision, Ellie wielded the halberd.

The halberd throbbed like a living thing in her hand. And when the enemy advanced toward her friends? The halberd bid her raise it, and then it struck out at all of the enemies at once, paralyzing man and horse alike. The kilted Camerons fell off their horses, crying out in injury. Their horses fell down in their own kind of panic.

This paralysis lasted only a moment, but it wreaked havoc. Enough so that the Murrays and her friends cried war and rushed the Camerons.

Even as Ellie saw the coveted victory in her mind, the halberd kept crooning to her. "Och darlin' love, we wull dae such miraculous things taegither. Dae ye want me? Aye, ye dae. Fight for me. Ye wull need tae get me away from her and then kill my previous owner."

Ellie doubted she could do that.

Her finger itched mercilessly.

The halberd's tone turned soft, sultry, even. "O' course she is strong, this druid child."

Panic welled up in Ellie. Tahra was a druid child! A magical creature! How could she ever prevail?

The itch in her finger became a burn, it was so intense.

The halberd's voice was calm, soothing, yet still beseeching. "Ne'er fear, my love. Syne ye hae a hand upon me, she canna use my magic agin ye. Hold on tight. 'Tis worth fighting for, I am."

The halberd showed himself freezing all of one previous owner's enemies in a loch. Him rousing a hornet's nest to engulf another's enemies. A third's enemies food poisoning them.

A thought came to Ellie against her will. What had happened to all the previous owners? Had the halberd convinced the next owner to kill them as well? She didn't want that to go on. She would just destroy the halberd and free up Ciaran from his crippling curse.

The halberd had heard her. "Och, nay. Ye shall na destroy me."

Ellie seized on what the halberd wasn't saying.

"Ye dinna deny that if I destroy ye, the curse o' crippling on Ciaran wull be lifted. This makes me all the maire determined, where yer wheedling did na."

That was one thing that happened when Ellie touched the halberd. It spoke to her, and she to it.

The other thing that happened at the same time, was Tahra woke up and grabbed onto the halberd as well. Even without the halberd's magic strength, the druid child was physically strong, tugging on the halberd one way while Ellie tugged on it the other way.

Tahra could hear what Ellie and the halberd were saying to each other in their minds. The druid child also could read Ellie's plan to destroy the halberd.

Ellie knew this, because Tahra's voice came into her head as well. "Let go, and I wull ainly kill ye. Hauld on, and I wull kill everyone ye e'er loved."

Neither of them spoke aloud.

Every bit of each moment, Ellie was tugging her hardest, digging her feet into the dirt to resist the tug of the other. She didn't dare waste any breath on speaking.

And fortunately for Ellie, she was strong enough to make Tahra save her breath, too, or a dozen guards would have already been in the tent with the two of them.

Ellie braced her foot against a heavy chest that sat on the ground in the tent. Amazed when it didn't drag away, she used it for leverage. She pushed down on her end of the halberd, forcing Tahra onto her toes to hold on to her own end. In seconds, Ellie would pry Tahra's hands loose. She would have the halberd. It would be hers.

Panic shone in the druid child's eyes, and she let some of the reasons come to the surface of her thoughts, where Ellie could see. Because of the magic of the halberd, Tahra hadn't gone back to nature and performed the periodic rituals to recover her own Druid magic. Without the halberd, she would be a normal warrior.

Not helpless, Ellie anew. She had seen Tahra fight Baltair with the sword. Still, without the halberd, the druid child wouldn't be striking down the Murray clan.

Ellie gathered all of her strength for one last push down. So close. She was so close to leveraging the halberd up out of Tahra's hands. She just needed to push a little harder.

In the back of Ellie's mind, she'd heard footsteps running. Guards yelling in the distance when they discovered the bound-up guard. But now a new noise came up. A noise that was near.

Oh well. In a second, she would have the halberd and be able to fight off whatever it was. She doubled down her effort to push, putting her weight into it. Straining. Growling. Just a little more.

With a whoosh of air, the side of the tent came up.

Baltair grabbed Ellie under the arms like a child and used her leverage to shove Tahra away. He hoisted Ellie up onto the horse with him, turned and galloped out of Cameron camp.

Ellie fumed. She'd been moments from having the halberd.

CHAPTER EIGHT

Ellie pounded on Baltair's arms. Cameron camp was racing by their hoof-pounding horse, even as torches began to light the darkness, with all of the Camerons waking from their pallets in the dead of night because of all the commotion.

Whether she wanted to or not, she had to grab hold of his waist and hang on for dear life. When she did, the warmth of him seeped into her, right through their woolen clothing. Being near him like this — enjoying the feeling— frustrated her. It was difficult to stay angry at someone you were hugging.

He was busy guiding the horse, but every now and then, his elbows would hug her arms around his waist. Just for a moment.

Soon, they had galloped clean out of camp and

were joined by Harold and Nadia, on Harold's horse. The trees between the two camps flew by now, as often as not coming between the two horses.

Whenever they could, Nadia's eyes met Ellie's, and Ellie saw the questions in them. A whole silent conversation passed between the two women.

"Ye did na get the halberd,"

"Nay, I did na, thanks tae Baltair's intrusion."

"Ye were in danger. He saved ye."

"I was sae close tae getting the halberd. Sae close tae saving yer husband."

"'Tis na yer duty tae save him. Let the men dae that. 'Tis glad I am all is right with ye."

They didn't slow one bit until they were back at Murray camp. Once they stopped the lathered and blowing horses, Harold's men came to greet him, swords and bows ready just in case.

Ciaran broke away from Connell, grabbed Nadia down off Harold's horse, and held her close in a fierce hug. "Tell me ye will na ever sneak off again. What did ye think tae dae? You had the whole clan worried."

Harold's men had all roused from sleep and were clapping him on the back and putting their arms around him. One after the other to the last man, he grasped forearms with them and put his hand on their shoulder, reassuring them. As he turned to lead them toward the planning fire between his and Searc's tents, he looked knowingly at Ellie.

What did it mean? Was he a time traveler after all?

Her attention was snapped back to Baltair, who was reaching out a hand. She took it.

Baltair gently helped her down from the horse, looking around at the few stragglers who were still nearby.

Connell led Baltair's horse away. Everyone else took the hint and found somewhere else to be, all except for Nadia and Ciaran, who still stood next to them, holding each other tight.

Ellie looked up at Baltair's earnest-to-the-point-of-stricken face. He really had been trying to help her. To save her life. "Baltair, I ken ye were just trying tae help, and sae I—"

"Ellie, how could ye sneak off in such a way? They could hae kidnapped ye. Tortured ye. Ye put the entire camp in danger!"

Really? He was going there?

She yelled to be heard over him, stomping her foot and standing as tall as she could. "How could ye, after I risked sae much, interrupt me right when I had my hand on the halberd? Ye ruinit everything! I was gaun'ae apologize, seeing as how ye thought tae save my life. Now I am madder than ever!"

Baltair scoffed. Looking exasperated, he raised his own voice that much higher. "There is na way on God's green waurld ye were gaun'ae hae that halberd. 'Tis magical! Tahra would hae used it agin ye, if ye were there but a moment longer!"

Whoa. The man had no faith in her at all.

Twisting the blasted ring that was making her finger itch, Ellie scoffed right back at him, quickly dipping her chin once for emphasis. "I verra wull ken what the halberd can dae. It spoke tae me. I was leveraging it oot o' Tahra's hands! One more second, and I would hae had it!"

Ciaran's voice, sad and pleading, interrupted her. "Baltair did save ye, then. Ye wull recall that using the halberd cost me my fighting legs."

He knocked the wind out of her sails.

Ellie slowed down a bit. Eyes on Ciaran, she explained, "I was gaun'ae destroy it with fire. Both the halberd and Tahra saw that in my mind, and neither o' them denied 'twould work."

Ciaran and Nadia both gave her sad smiles of thanks for the effort before turning back to hug each other warm in the cold night.

Baltair got in her face, lecturing. "Dinna gae

recklessly throwing yer life away again, because I wull likely try again tae save ye, sae invested am I in yer wull-being." His face was angry, but more at himself.

She could tell, because his eyes on her were tender, and his tone was full of restraint. What did he wish he could do? She should drop it.

Her finger itched again, blast the thing. She pulled the ring up and fiercely scratched her finger, then bristled and turned away from Baltair. Who did he think he was, ordering her around? Mom had fought often with Dad over just this need to control, and it had killed them both.

Nadia took Ellie by the hand and led her by moonlight through Murray camp toward her and Ciaran's tent. "Come. We all need sleep, and ye need tae get away from him before ye say some aught ye regret."

Heart swelling with gratitude, Ellie smiled and followed, leaving Ciaran to talk Baltair down.

Nadia hugged her. "All wull be right. Ye wull see."

For some stupid reason, this made Ellie cry. It was a deep cry, the kind that made her throat ache so that she could barely speak. But she had a strong urge to explain. To have one person who understood just how close she had come. "I had it in my hand! Why did he have to interrupt?"

Nadia opened the tent flap and gestured for Ellie to go in, then followed her and made room for the two of them to sit on Ellie's pallet.

Sitting with Nadia like this made Ellie miss Baltair. How could that be, when she was so angry at him, so frustrated?

Nadia put a reassuring hand on Ellie's arm. "I hae ne'er seen ye sae worked up aboot anything. Why does this bother ye sae?"

Ellie took a deep breath and let it out, then snuggled up against her friend. "My parents."

Nadia was hesitant. "Yer parents?"

"Dad treated Mom more like property than someone he loved. Barking orders. She left him ower it."

"That's tough. How old were ye?"

"I was fourteen when they divorced, fifteen when their fighting kilt them both."

Nadia jumped a bit at this, and her eyes opened wide. "Kilt them both! What dae ye mean?"

Ellie waved a hand to try and calm her friend. "It was my first day o' high school. They both wanted tae take me, sae we all went taegither in Mom's Audi. They argued the whole way. He said she should hae dressed me more ladylike. She said 'twas none o' his business. He said I was still his daughter. And on, and on, and on. When they dropped me off at school, they both made like they were smiling at me. But really, they were each seething at the other. Dad insisted he should drive. Said that unlike her, he knew what he was doing. Mom threw her hands up and said, 'Gae on then, yer Lairdship.' I shook my head and walked away. What were they thinking, getting in the car together? There wasn't enough room for the two of them in such a small space. I had been relieved, back when they got divorced, because the yelling had stopped. Anyway, that first day at high school was the last time I saw them alive. They crashed the car and died while I sat in first period French. I had tae gae live with Granny in North Carolina. At least they taught Gaelic there."

"I dinna ken what tae say," Nadia admitted. "Wull, I dae wish tae say some aught. Ye ken it was na yer fault, aye?"

Ellie barked a laugh, but at the same time, she squeezed her friend's hand. "Aye, I ken it was na my fault. That's the first thing everybody asks me. Dinna fash. I ken ye are trying tae help, and I appreciate it. Nay, fault is na why it bothers me sae."

"Being withoot them would bother ye nay matter what the reason why."

"Och, aye, 'twould. But what bothers me about it the most is they could na e'en stop fighting long enough tae pay attention tae the road, ye ken?"

"I can see why being bossed around chaps yer hide sae. I dinna like it either. Fortunately, Ciaran does na dae it."

"He's crippled now, but supposedly he was a great warrior, per Harold Cochran's version o' things."

"Aye, he was verra good at fighting. Ye saw it yerself."

Ellie was on her way to a breakthrough. Her mind told her so. She just couldn't put her finger on it yet. She kept ruminating along the lines of their discussion. "My father was na warrior. Far from it. He worked on the assembly line."

And then Nadia spoke the breakthrough Ellie was headed toward. She said it offhand, as if it weren't important. "Mayhap Baltair wishes he were maire o' a warrior than he is. Mayhap yer Dad did tae."

Ellie balked at the significance of that, but all she said was, "Mayhap."

Nadia's next whisper was calm, but hesitant. "I

hae some aught tae say, but I fear ye wull be angered and na talking tae me, much as ye are na talking tae Baltair. Wull ye hear me oot?"

Ellie put a hand on her friend's arm to make her look at her.

It worked. The look on Nadia's face stunned Ellie. Nadia was afraid, really afraid.

Ellie wrinkled her brow in confusion, but kept her voice to a whisper, as well. "What has ye sae frightened? What hae I e'er done tae cause ye tae doubt me?"

Nadia rubbed her face for a moment, took a breath and let it out, then whispered with obvious trepidation. "Ev'r syne ye found that ring and put it on, ye hae been a hundrit times maire reckless. I think it has magic in it. Druid magic. Who kens, mayhap it allows them tae hear us. Ye should take it off, Ellie. Bury it deep in the ground far away from here."

Ellie relaxed. "Is that all? Wull I ken, already. I thought ye were gaun'ae tell me aught fearsome!"

Nadia laughed softly, and Ellie joined her.

It wasn't until Nadia had been looking at her expectantly a few moments that Ellie realized she actually expected her to take the ring off. And leave it behind.

"Och nay," she whispered to Nadia. "I ken I should, but then where would I be? This ring is the ainly thing making me brave enough tae exist at all in this time. Withoot it, I would hae been begging Eoin tae take me haime lang syne."

CHAPTER NINE

B altair watched Ellie go off with Nadia. He didn't realize how tense his body was until Ciaran came over and put a hand on his back.

"Ye can unclench yer fists. There is na enemy here tae fight."

"Why does na she listen? 'Twill be the death o' the lass, if she stays here in oor time."

Ciaran tapped Baltair's arm and beckoned him walk a bit up the mountain with him, above the camp.

Baltair nodded, holding his cousin's elbow to help him limp along on the flat ground and giving him an arm up as they climbed. Once they are up and out of earshot, he turned around and looked down at the camp below. A few campfires still burned, but most of the Murrays had gone back to their sleeping pallets. Ciaran and Nadia's tent was dark, but he imagined the lasses whispering with each other, even as he and Ciaran were speaking.

Ciaran followed his gaze and nodded. "They call themselves 'modern women'."

"Modern women? Whatever dae they mean?"

"Mostly, that they are able tae dae anything a man can dae."

Baltair laughed, looking for Ciaran to join him.

But Ciaran didn't. Instead, he looked at Baltair expectantly.

Baltair wrinkled his brow and squinted his eyes, looking for any signs that his cousin was daft. "O' course there are things men can dae which the lasses canna."

Ciaran gave an inpatient shake of his head. "And things which ainly lasses can dae, such as bearing bairns. But we are na talking aboot that. The lasses live in a time that is less warlike, ye ken. There are nay battles. Neither o' them has seen a one. All that needs doing is building goods and getting those goods tae market. Ye dae ken anyone can dae that, aye?"

Baltair felt trapped. If he admitted that, then there was going to be another step he would have to admit. And another. So he said nothing.

Ciaran nudged him with his elbow. "In their time 'tis true. Lasses and men share the work equally."

"Ye canna believe that. What aboot heavy work?"

"Nadia says they hae machines for the heavy work, lifting and whatnot. 'Tis truly a verra different time. Howsoever, ye are in the right aboot one thing.""

Relief swept through Baltair. He'd been on the cusp of losing his cousin forever, into some sort of madness. Perhaps there was a chance to save him yet. "Aye? Dae tell me. What am I in the right aboot?"

"The lasses dinna ken what they're aboot when it comes tae battle, fighting, and warriors. They had na business, being ower in the enemy's camp. I dinna ken what got intae Ellie, but I wull talk with Nadia aboot keeping it oot o' her. For all oor sakes."

* * *

IN THE MORNING, BALTAIR AGAIN GRABBED TWO cups of mash and took them over to Ciaran's tent. "Ellie, coome on oot for practice. I brought ye aught tae break yer fast."

"What time is it?" she called out from inside in a croaky voice.

Ciaran's voice came from the other side of the tent. "'Tis way past time ye were up."

Nadia's laugh came wafting over the tent, as well. "Aye, sleepyhead. Get up!"

There was a rustling inside the tent, and then Ellie's squinty-eyed face appeared through the flap, followed by her rumpled self. At least she had her clothes on.

Baltair handed her one of the cups of mash and walked her to where the cups needed to be turned in. They ate in silence. That done, he walked her over to the practice area. "Choose yer ain practice weapon this time. Ken for certies 'tis the right size for ye, and has balance."

She mumbled something as she did so, but she did a good job of it, hefting each practice sword for its weight and then holding it by the handle to test its balance.

It made him proud.

She selected one, well-balanced and the perfect length for her height, and ran toward him, brandishing it with a huge smile. "'Tis surprised I am, that ye still want tae teach me."

He crouched, ready to parry as he had shown her. "Did na ye ken I would honor my promise?"

She stopped and put the sword tip down in the dirt with a frown. "Och, nay. 'Twas na that."

He raised his sword high in the air and waited for her to raise hers to block it, smiling encouragement when she did.

She held as firm as she could to block his blow, but she was obviously not strong enough to do it.

He threw his practice sword on the ground and gestured for her to join him over on the sidelines. After she ran over, he showed her the motion he would use to step aside and avoid an attack, then explained as much while he backed away.

Smiling with altogether too much joy, she raised her practice sword and ran at him in a charge, laughing when he moved and she blew by him, then stopping on the sidelines to lean forward and put her hands on her thighs.

When at last he could no longer put off asking what was on his mind, he spoke in the same calm manner he always used when it was his turn to teach the wee ones. "Why then were ye surprised?"

She had to huff a dozen breaths before she was able to speak. "The way ye were gang on last night, I thought ye did na want anything tae dae with me. I thought ye would insist Eoin take me haime sae that I never bothered yer clan again."

He gave her a sheepish smile. "I was na sae vicious as all that, was I?"

She put her hands on her hips, comically poking the practice sword out behind her as lass would a stirring spoon. "Aye, ye were."

He raised his practice sword high and made as if to run at her, then raised his chin to tell her to get ready to move aside. When she did, he charged and spoke at the same time, just to show her it could be done. "Wull, as I took it on tae teach ye, ye are my responsibility."

Not only did she get out of the way, but also she swung the practice sword hard at his head.

He easily ducked, but he could tell she was genuinely angry. "Whoa, lass. That would hae taken my head off."

She ran at him again, sword raised to do some damage this time, but when he easily moved aside, she stopped and panted, glaring at him. "Just because I'm a lass who spake tae ye, a man, does na make me yer responsibility."

Instead of raising his ire, as they would have last night, Ellie's words drew his attention to how hard she was trying to learn the fighting moves, even though she was in terrible physical condition. Ciaran had been right to tell him what he had, dear man.

To let her catch her breath, he just stood there breathing himself. When he was sure she could speak with decorum, he said, "'Tis nay because I am a man, but rather because I ken the Highland ways. Ye are my guest, sae 'tis my duty tae teach ye."

She was thinking it over, because her lips pressed tightly together, and she looked the other way a moment. When she turned back to him, she had regained her composure. "Today ye hae been kinder. If ye continue tae dae sae, I suppose I can abide yer teaching." Moving with exaggerated slowness, she attacked.

Matching her slowness, he side-stepped her attack.

She watched where his feet moved.

He didn't want to smile and give away how proud he was of her, but since it was happening anyway, he told her as he slowly raised his own sword up to attack. "Aye. That be the way o' it."

She slowly stepped aside now, ducking as his sword came up and slowly moving her own sword up to attack and stepping to the side to avoid his blow and moving to the side again to give her own blow.

Round and round they went, gradually matching each other's slow movements, one attacking while the other side stepped.

Her eyes never left his, all the while. Truth be told, their faces were getting closer and closer together.

It was unlike any fight he had ever been in, but he certainly wasn't going to move away from her.

Ciaran's voice called out from the sidelines, "Bed her and be done with it!"

Ellie dissolved into laughter even as Baltair did, her red cheeks saying she was just as embarrassed as he was, at being observed in such a strangely intimate moment.

He gave Ciaran a grateful look though. His cousin's usual charming way had broken the tension between Baltair and Ellie.

They spent the rest of their practice time productively, without arguing. The midday meal was pleasant, with Ellie, Ciaran, and Nadia all around him, carefully not speaking of the battle to come soon and instead speaking of pleasantries. They had more productive practice in the afternoon — though they never did get face to face again.

When it came time for the evening meal, everyone in the Murray camp gathered around the fire again, between Searc and Raild's tents. The stew they ate was wondrous, because Eoin, Connell and some of Raild's men had gone hunting. The mood therefore was high, as everyone ate their fill of meat.

Raild took the spot by the fire then, where everyone could see his face as he walked around and around it, looking them all in the eye by turns. "A belly full o' meat on the day before battle bodes well for the body." He waited for that to sink in, listening while the murmurs surged and died down. "Aye. We canna sit by and allow the Camerons tae call in maire allies and supplies. We need tae attack tomorrow." He said more.

But Baltair could tell Ellie stopped listening when she realized how soon Baltair's life was going to be in danger. He saw it in her eyes, how terrified she was for him. He wanted to throw his arm around her shoulders and draw her close, but he didn't know if she would chew his head off, or what.

Raild called for his fiddle, and there was dancing.

Baltair stood with Ellie, watching for a time. In truth, he was watching her. She watched the dancing with such rapt attention, a man would think she had never seen dancing before. She was like this with everything, and she made him feel more alive.

He led her over to where the dishes were being gathered. They got rid of theirs, and then he turned to her and nodded his head in as courtly a fashion as he could manage. "Will ye give me the pleasure o' a dance, Ellie?"

She flipped her hand over so her palm was to the sky. "'Tis aboot time ye asked. I thought ye ne'er would." Smiling, she took both his hands and skipped with him over into the dance set.

CHAPTER TEN

B altair was breathless. The firelight made Ellie's ginger hair shine like gold. His gaze was drawn by the way it bounced as she danced. How her eyes sparkled in the moonlight. Even more, he was pleased by her interest in his family. She asked question after question about the MacGregor clan, whenever the dance set brought her back to him. Most of her questions were safe, but once in a while she got carried away.

"Sae Connell and Eoin's grand da was ye and Ciaran's great, great, great, great someaught?" she asked as he spun her around by the elbow.

He switched elbows and spinning directions, leaning in to speak to her softly. "Whisht. I dinna think Raild's men ken aboot time travel."

She took his offered hand, and everyone in the set skipped twice toward each other in a circle. "Ye dinna? Seems they would be the first tae ken."

"Wull," he said as they skipped back again, "I would na be the one who telt it tae those who dinna ken, would ye?"

"Nay." She lowered her voice to the barest whisper and put her face up close to his ear as they stood and clapped, watching another pair dance patterns alone in the center of the set. "Sae did I get it right?"

Her breath in his ear did alarming things to his body that he didn't want her to be aware of, yet he couldn't resist responding in kind, leaning close to her own ear. "Aye, ye got it right."

He was separated from Ellie for a bit while they turned elbows with everyone else, going opposite directions around the circle.

She was back at his side, smiling and clapping. "Hae ye heard any news o' Meehall, Sarah, and Meehall's children?"

Frowning, he shook his head no, then leaned up against her ear again. "Nay, Eoin says it is na safe tae talk tae Kelsey in oor dreams any maire. He telt her tae quit."

When he said that, she looked at the ring on her

right finger with a worried look on her face for several long moments, interrupting her clapping. But then she came back to him from whatever had been on her mind, smiling up at him bravely. "'Tis glad I am tae be here with ye this evening, dang this dance. I'm having fun."

He let himself smile a genuine smile and show her for once just how much he enjoyed her company. "I'm having fun as wull, and I'm glad ye are here."

The dance took her away, but she was back often enough that they kept talking without too much trouble.

"Are ye acquainted with any other MacGregors?"

"Nay, ainly Eoin, Connell, Ciaran, and Meehall. I did know Ciaran's Da afore he died. He was my Da's brother."

"Did ye know their parents?"

"Nay, dae ye see any great grand das in the war party?"

She looked about only briefly and then back to him. "Nay, I dinna. Hae all the grand das passed away, then?"

The sadness in her face shamed him. He gave her a reassuring shake of the head. "They dinna stay in the war camp, ye ken. They gae tae one o' the Murray castles as pensioners, working oot their aulder days as stable hands or kitchen maids. In safety and relative ease."

"I'm glad," she told him.

Every time her conversation ran out of steam like this, the dance would put the energy back in her, and she returned to him with questions or jests about a new topic. She was enchanting. Refreshing. Full of life. Just what he needed the eve before a battle. It was hard, remembering he was not what she needed. She needed someone who could keep her in a safe place, far away from everything that would happen on the morrow.

His face must have revealed his worry, because Eoin met his eye and glanced furtively toward the horses, then at Ellie and nodded his head. His meaning was clear. He would get her away when the time came. They had already discussed getting Ciaran and Nadia back to the safety of Celtic University before the battle started.

Baltair glanced to make sure Ellie was looking the other way, then gave his cousin a slight bow of his head, in thanks.

Ellie came back, sparkling with a new thought. "Hae ye been tae a castle? Tae the one Sarah lives in now?"

He stifled the amused smile that threatened to

break out, knowing she would feel insulted. "Aye, we all hae been there. We gae for the feasts at Christmas and Midsummer."

Her eyes danced along with her feet, clearly caught up in a fantasy. "What's it like? Is it grand?"

"Aye, 'tis grand. And oor current Laird runs it as a family. Calls us each by name. 'Tis a wonder he remembers us all, if ye ask me."

"What's his lady like?"

"She is... maire concerned with the lives o' her ain children than oors. But that is as it should be."

Ellie laughed. "I see ye are a diplomat as well as a warrior."

"Aye, that I am. Every Highlander needs tae be."

"Is that true?"

"Aye, 'tis, but na in the way ye think. We dinna all make treaties. Leave it tae the parliament tae cock that up. Join with England? How can they think that best? Howsoever, we see folk from other clans nearly daily. A wrong word can put lives in danger..." He was carried away by the speech he was making, until he looked at her face and remembered just how close she'd come to losing her own life in the Cameron camp just the day before. "'Tis sorry I—"

She interrupted to make light of his error, as was her way when she preferred not to think of things seriously. "Dinna worry yer pretty head aboot it." Away she went, skipping around the circle with a new set of dancers, throwing her all into it, red hair flying and skirts flapping to the beat of Raild's fiddle. She was beautiful, the embodiment of spirit.

She put in so much effort to cover up how deep her thoughts ran. Should he tell her he saw right through it?

No.

No, that would ruin her charm. Unselfconscious as she was now, she was a delight. He needed to be more careful about not bringing up hurtful memories for her. Not rub her nose in her wrong decisions. Having done this made him no better than a bad war chief. Before Searc, Murray Clan had someone like that. He had run Baltair and Ciaran's fathers into their graves. Needlessly.

She was back to him again. "Sae what dae the children, in the castle? If the men are stable hands and the women work in the kitchen, are the children allowed tae play outside? Hae they toys?"

He didn't know what she was getting at, so he just answered frankly. "Aye, the children gae ootside and play with toy swords and toy bows. Both lads and lasses. I can recall many mock battles on the courtyard of the castle when I was a lad, along with Ciaran and many others who are na longer here—"

She cut him off before he said more about those who had died. He was grateful. What was he thinking?

She kept him on the subject that interested her, rather than the subject she was really asking about. "Hae the children other toys besides weapons? Dae the lasses play with dolls? Tea sets?"

That made him laugh. "Tea sets?"

She abruptly stopped clapping along with the fiddle and put her hands on her hips. "Aye, tea sets. Lasses in my time hae lovely tea parties, with all o' oor dolls and anyone else who wull play along."

He raised his eyebrows, both to show his surprise and to apologize for making fun of her. "Wull, the lasses o' this time dinna hae their ain tea sets. If they lay hands on one, then 'tis tae help set the table."

"Och, that's a shame. Dae they hae dolls, at least?"

"Aye, they hae dolls."

"What are the dolls made o', wood?"

"A few are made o' wood. Most o' cloth."

"Dae the parents e'er play with their children? Or are the children expected tae keep their ain company and stay away from adult business?"

"Ne'er shall it be sae. The adults teach the children adult business. Na ainly swords and bows, but alsae washing, cooking, and tending tae livestock. Lads and lasses dae their share o' the chores as soon as they are able. I remember being watched by several grand das. I always liked that better."

She let out a merry laugh that lit up her face. "I would like tae see a grand da oot in the castle courtyard, running aboot with the children and their toy bows and swords. Lovely."

They danced every dance, but Raild at last stopped playing his fiddle.

Baltair walked Ellie to Ciaran and Nadia's, pausing when they arrived in the shadow the tent made in the moonlight. The Scottish skies were still clear, and all the stars shone down on them like fairy magic, bouncing their light off the leaves of the trees, it was so bright.

He couldn't help staring at Ellie's face. It was unbearably beautiful, framed by hair glowing with starshine. "I hope ye pass as good a night as we had an evening, Ellie. Thank ye for the dances."

She smiled with a question in her eyes, an invitation.

He moved in close to her, but he gave her a quick hug instead of a kiss. "Good night, Ellie."

"Good night Baltair," she said with a puzzled look on her face as she opened the flap and went inside the tent, where Ciaran and Nadia could be heard talking softly.

On Baltair's way back to his own tent, he noticed Raild, Searc, and all the warriors were gathered around the fire again. As usual during a meeting of the clan, the drummers were doing their best to conceal what was being said from listeners out in the heather.

Baltair took a seat next to Connell, who gave him a nod and then turned back to hear what was being said.

"'Tis a shipment o' supplies, most likely weapons. We need someone tae size up their defenses."

Baltair stood and raised his voice to be heard. "I wull gae."

Searc came over and clasped forearms with Baltair. "Ye must leave right away. 'Twas seen on the south road."

"Verra wull," Baltair told his clan's war chief before he turned and ran toward where his horse was tied up with the other horses. This was his chance to prove himself. To gain more of Searc's trust. The Murray war chief would then put him in a more prominent place in the battle tomorrow. Baltair could get some of the glory. He wouldn't just be one of the background fighters who didn't get any mention in the songs and legends.

Such as Raild's book about Ciaran.

Baltair was reaching up to untie his horse when Ellie ran up and grabbed his arm, speaking so fast she sounded like a child. "Where dae ye gae in such a state? I thought ye had taken tae yer pallet. Why are ye up in the middle o' the night? Wull ye take me with ye?"

He was firm with her, as befitted a warrior being sent on a mission. "Nay, ye canna coome along. Dinna fash. I wull be careful."

Before he realized what he was doing, he kissed Ellie on the mouth. It was the sort of kiss a husband gives his wife before he goes off to battle, sweet and loving but also promising and demanding.

He pulled away, silently chiding himself. He shouldn't encourage her affections.

Ellie was staring at him, looking as dazed as he felt. After a few long moments, her eyes met his, looking thrilled. This look changed to puzzlement when he didn't say anything.

Well, that couldn't be helped. Best just to get on with what he needed to do. He untied the horse, got on, and rode away. Were his feelings so strong that he could no longer control himself? His mind kept reminding him what he'd just done, to the beat of the horse's hooves as he trotted away.

It wasn't far to a good place to look out over the south road. When he got close, he slowed down but stayed in the trees, in the shadows of the moon and starlight.

The horse reached down to graze, and he let it have its head, glad for it to be occupied and not wanting to run, as it often did when it had been tied up all day. He peered through the trees down to the road.

Sure enough, there was a shipment of goods. And yes, it included a cannon. If the Murrays could stop the shipment, that would be best. But it was heavily guarded. He noted a dozen Cameron warriors. He needed to go back and get more people, so he reached down the horse's neck to grab the reins.

Hands grabbed Baltair's legs and pulled him off the horse.

He slapped the horse and watched it run back toward Murray camp.

CHAPTER ELEVEN

Cursing under her breath, Ellie scratched at the knot tying Ciaran's horse next to where Baltair's horse had been. After one failed attempt, she mounted just in time to follow Baltair out of the campsite. If she hurried, she wouldn't lose sight of him. There he went, straight south past the warriors' fire. She would prefer not to let them see her following him, but oh well.

None of the men called out to her. In her time, she would expect some catcalls. Here, she got nothing. Didn't they see her?

Wait, why did she care? She had better things to worry about.

Baltair was entering the trees. If she let him get

too far ahead, he would lose her in the forest. She squeezed the horse tighter with her knees. There, she was catching up to Baltair.

He had to slow down when he entered the trees, lest the horse trip on a root —or worse, go under a low lying branch that would knock its rider off its back.

Now, following him was easy. She stayed back far enough so that he wouldn't overhear her over his own horse's hoofbeats, but if he looked back, he'd see her instantly. That would be the end of this outing for her, wouldn't it. Hm, maybe not. Would he take the time to make her go back to camp? She smiled. She didn't think so.

Baltair rode through the forest around the mountain in the same direction she and Nadia had gone, but in a more southerly arc. He stopped on the edge of the forest overlooking a grassy canyon between the two mountains, concentrating on a road down there.

She pulled back on her horse's reins and let her legs go loose, just in time to be quiet and not draw his attention. Afraid he might look back and see her, she turned this way and that, looking for a place she might hide. There was nothing close. Moving right now would probably draw attention to her anyway. The idea brought back sweet memories of Grandpa.

* * *

AFTER HER PARENTS DIED IN THE CAR CRASH, Grandpa and Gran took Ellie in. They lived clear across the country —in another universe, to fifteen-year-old Ellie. She grew up in the city, taking the bus to the bookstore whenever she wanted. Gran and Grandpa lived on a small farm, twenty miles from the nearest town.

Too young to drive on her own, Ellie studied and got her learner's permit the first week she was there, but that still meant Grandpa had to be in the car with her.

Grandpa was more patient than she'd ever imagined a man could be, after the way Dad had been. So driven, both for himself and for everyone around him.

When Ellie went to Jefferson High School that first Monday, she found out the freshman and sophomore mothers had a small bus and would carpool student clubs on field trips on the weekends. She would join all the clubs!

But compared to her high school back in the city that had 2000 students, Jefferson only had 200 students. On a good day. And they started high school in ninth grade, unlike back at home where they started in tenth. The number and variety of clubs Jefferson had were small.

One day, Ellie was trying to switch the antique gear shift on the old pickup truck she had to learn driving in. She ground the gears, of course, a terrible sound.

Grandpa didn't sigh, didn't say a thing. He just sat patiently by, waiting for her to get it right. God bless the man.

After two weeks of this, he ventured to say something. Sometimes. He always spoke as if he cared. "What's got your mind so occupied, Ellie girl?"

If he had been cross or demanding, she would've tuned him out, just like she had tuned out Dad. But Grandpa was so patient, it motivated her.

Before she knew it, she was telling him, "I was all excited about joining the movie club so I could go to town every Saturday night, watch two movies, and have that count for school spirit points. But there's too many kids in that club already. The bus is already full."

Without saying a word, he leaned forward and put his finger on the spot where she had to shift in order to put the truck in first gear and get going down this street before the car behind them got too close and embarrassed her.

With a quick smile at him, she managed to do it this time and got started off the stop sign before the other car pulled up behind her. They were the only two cars in sight, and she didn't want to know who was in there, or for them to know she was the one who couldn't manage to get going off the stop sign.

He winked at her, a reward for getting the job done. "I could take you to the movie theater every Saturday, Ellie girl."

She wiped a tear from her eye with her left hand while keeping her right hand firmly on the steering wheel. "That's so nice of you. Thank you."

"It's nothing, sugar."

"I'm not finished. Your sweetness has me crying, but I had more to say."

"Well, spit it out, honey child."

"That's nice of you, but it defeats the purpose. Yes, I wanted to see the movies and have them count for spirit points, but I also wanted to be with the other kids. If I arrive separately, the kids in the bus will already have decided who they're going to sit next to. It'll be awkward for me, trying to join them. I'd rather not bother with it now. But thank you, from the depths of my heart."

"You're welcome, Ellie girl. There's got to be

some clubs you could join and hang out with them other kids, aren't there?"

They were coming up on another stop sign, and she had to pay attention to just how hard to put her foot on the brake so that the truck wouldn't stop before it got there but wouldn't go past the sign, either.

At first, she pushed too hard, and it stalled.

Grandpa patiently jumped in with instruction. "Put your foot on the clutch, Ellie, quick. That's it. Now slowly shift right here where my finger is. Good. Now shift it into first gear. There you go. Now brake."

Ellie gave him a pained smile. "I guess someone who knows what they're doing really should be in the car with someone who's learning how to drive."

"Mmmmm," was all he said. Not "I told you so."

Now she had to start again from a stop. She moved her finger surreptitiously to the area where she thought she had to hit the cranky old gearshift first, before it would go into first gear.

Just as surreptitiously, he moved her hand forward a bit, then quickly let go while still looking out the window, ostensibly admiring the neighbor's fields.

Pleased with herself, she got it on the first try this time and was underway before that car came up behind her. "All the clubs with room are things I don't know how to do. Fishing. Hunting."

"How do you feel about fishing and hunting?" he asked her while still looking at the fields, his voice mild. No pressure at all.

"I don't know how I feel about them. Like I told you, I don't have any idea how."

He chuckled. "Now, Ellie girl. I mean, are you one of them people who can't abide the idea of killing animals or fish?"

Oh. He was aware of what was going on in the world outside the farm. "No," she told him matter-of-factly. "So long as it's eaten, I see no problem with getting free-range meat instead of feedlot meat at the market."

He chuckled again and slapped his knee. "Good, Ellie girl. Good, good, good. Well, hunting comes with a whole bunch of precautions you'd need to learn. If you want, we'll go down that trail. But fishing? Fishing is something I can teach you in one day. If you want."

Joy surfaced in Ellie's mind for the first time since her parents died. She stopped at the next stop sign effortlessly and restarted just so. "Would you teach me to fish? I think I'd like that."

"'Course. We'll go out first thing Saturday morning. When we get home, we'll take a look at all my tackle and find some that suits you. And if you like fishing, I'll buy you your own."

They had arrived at the market. She parked the car and hugged him. "I'll be proud to use your stuff, Grandpa. So proud. That'll be better than having my own."

She looked forward to that Saturday's fishing trip. When the day finally came, the two of them headed out to the lake together with their fishing poles over their shoulders. Put all their things in the rowboat.

He pushed it off and rowed them to the middle of the lake. Showed her how to put a worm on her hook and cast out into the water. Cautioned her to be quiet.

She had a question, so she whispered, "Now what, Grandpa?"

He took a sip of the iced tea Gran had given him for the trip. "Now," he whispered back to her, "we stay as quiet as we can and hope the fish don't notice we're here."

* * *

Oh no. Baltair was so intent on watching the road down in the grassy canyon below, he didn't see those Camerons sneaking up on foot behind him.

The itch on Ellie's finger took up violently, giving her the urge to charge over and tell those Camerons to unhand her man.

She knew that was ridiculous. They were dragging Baltair off his horse, and if she showed herself, they would get her, too. Gritting her teeth against the hypnotic pull of the druid ring's magic, she yanked if off her finger and threw it as hard as she could into the forest, sending a flock of birds into flight.

The itching instantly stopped. So did the urge to charge off into harm's way.

Rational now, she turned around as quickly as she could manage the horse and urged him into a run back toward Murray camp. Let those Camerons hear her. Let them know someone would be coming after him. So long as they didn't catch her and prevent her from getting help.

She let the horse pick the way back through the trees. He would be anxious to get back to his herd, right? All she did was urge him on faster –but not too fast.

The way back seemed longer than it had on the way out here. The moon and stars gave great light, but she had no idea where she was going. She'd always heard that horses headed back to the barn, and she assumed the same thing was true about heading back to the herd. The longer it took her to get back there, the more she wondered if that was really true.

She saw the first few tents of Murray camp in the distance through the trees. At the same time, she heard the drumbeats that disguised their battle planning.

"Thank you, boy," she told the horse as it brought her right up to the clump of warriors.

A few of them turned around to look at her expectantly.

She searched through the faces until she found Eoin and addressed him. "Baltair's been captured!"

Eoin jumped up immediately, making eye contact with a few other warriors, who also jumped up to follow him. Among those was Connell. In moments, they were headed toward the horses, with Eoin turning to ask her, "Where did this happen?"

She stayed on Ciaran's horse and followed them. "At the edge of the trees overlooking the south road. There is a shipment of goods, and it does have a cannon. I saw it. But the Camerons must have been watching for us to come spy on them, because they grabbed him right off his horse."

Just as she was saying that, Baltair's horse ran up and stopped there, tossing its head and flapping its tail.

Right behind Baltair's horse came Harold. His face was stormy, and while he wasn't running, he was walking briskly, with authority. A dozen of his men followed him, blocking the way she had come.

Eoin and his men got on their horses and turned toward were Baltair had gone.

Harold put the palm of his hand out toward them. "Ye canna gae after him. They wull hae reached their camp by now. 'Tis tae risky. We must consider Baltair already lost." He stood there and watched them, clearly expecting them to dismount and put their horses away. He ignored Ellie.

Eoin plainly didn't agree with Harold. Raising his chin defiantly, he nodded to his men, then led them around the tents instead of past Harold and his men. "Fortunately for us," he called out to Harold, "we dinna take orders from ye."

Ellie rode over to where Ciaran had tied his horse up.

"Come on, Ellie," Eoin called out.

She looked over. He had stopped and was waiting for her.

CHAPTER TWELVE

J ust inside the tree line overlooking the grass and grey rock of a Highlands canyon, Baltair's hands were tied behind his back. His ankles were tied together, and he was thrown over the back of a Cameron horse. Tied there, his head bounced against the horse's belly all the way down the hill to the road, and then on the road as well, where those who had captured him joined the shipment caravan. His mouth had not been gagged, and the Cameron riders made sport of conversing with him.

"Sae ye thought tae gain oor cannon, eh?" one of them teased. It sounded like Dougal Cameron, but it could have been his brother, Brian. It was hard to tell with all the blood rushing to Baltair's up-side-down head.

Baltair kept quiet. They were already gloating over this, and the answer was obvious. He had nothing at all to gain from saying anything.

"Och," said a second Cameron, and this time Baltair was sure who it was. Airril had been spotted scouting near Murray camp the day before. "Ye wull forgive the lad. He's bit taxed for words just now. Allow him tae get the lay o' the land."

"Aye, give him a moment tae gather his wits aboot him," said Machar Cameron, to general laughter.

Teàrlach joined in on their sport with "As if he had any tae begin with!" raising the general noise of their laughter up a notch on the measuring stick.

Baltair's head was pounding with headache by now, and he closed his eyes, trying to escape as if into sleep. But the pain was worse this way.

Teàrlach rejoined with "What dae ye hope tae get by sending yer horse back?"

Baltair already saw red because of all the blood rushing to his head, but now anger strengthened him. He had held back curses against these Camerons for their taunting, but he couldn't help answering this last question. "I ainly hope tae keep my horse or anything else o' value away from the likes o' ye."

They all laughed heartily at him, making cut ups that all amounted to "Bet ye wish ye had him now."

Baltair's wind was being knocked out of him by the bouncing of the horse against his chest and by his head hanging down, but he forced himself to answer, "I am ainly glad one o' ye does na hae him."

A younger Cameron urged his horse right along-side Baltair, so he could look him in the eye when he demanded to know, "Ye would deny us everything, would ye?"

Baltair narrowed his eyes at the lad, which was ridiculous from Baltair's position as a trussed up captive but had the desired effect anyway.

The lad shut his gob.

Baltair stared the lad down. "I ainly deny ye the use o' Murray land. Ye Camerons hae yer ain lands. Why would ye deny the Murrays the use o' theirs? Dinna answer that. I ken why."

One of the older Camerons shooed the lad away out of sight, then addressed his kinsmen.

"Think ye he wull change his tune once he gets tae camp?"

"O' course he wull. How could he na?"

When they got to the enemy camp, several Camerons spat on Baltair's helpless face as the horse he was trussed to passed by. Savages, the Camerons were. They didn't take him down off the horse and allow him to walk like a man. No, they had to parade him through their camp like an animal to the slaughter.

They brought him to a small glade of trees on the edge of their camp, where Tahra held court in her white druid robe, with a crown of Rowan leaves on her blonde head. The halberd which had cursed Ciaran rested on her shoulder. She spoke of the oddest things, and Baltair only understood one word in five that she uttered as if blowing smoke.

Hanging on her every word were twelve slightly older and more heavyset kilted Highlanders with gray hair and more gold decoration than the other men had.

Trussed to a horse like prey turned to game, Baltair had the druid child's full attention when he arrived and was put before her in the center of this half circle of men.

She gave him a sinister smile as she stood there amid the trees and the flowers that should have made her beautiful. The contrast between their innocent beauty and her wicked scowl only showed how evil she was. And confident. So confident. With a gesture, she bade the warriors who had brought her to back away behind their leaders.

They did so instantly, as if her hand controlled their movement, clearing the ground between her face and Baltair's.

She stood tall and proud. The delivery of her words was haughty. "How ye must be cursing yerself tae the grave, for na allowing yer lass tae fight yer battle for ye and win. She was sae close. Why did ye stop her? She had her hands on the prize." She stroked the halberd as if it were her hair, then smiled cruelly. "Ye did na ken she was close tae obtaining it, did ye? Nay, ye did na believe a lass could dae it. What a fool ye hae been. And now they tell me ye were dragged off yer horse as ye sat with anither prize in sight. Ye are na worthy."

Her minions chuckled, but only half-heartedly, almost as if they had been told they must chuckle, but found no actual humor in what she had said.

With a flash of her evil eyes, Tahra twirled and had the halberd in her hands, raising it up toward the treetops all around them.

Lightning flashed overhead, causing the gold decorations on the Cameron men to shine with extra brightness, which was reflected in Tahra's grey eyes. Frightening. Compelling.

He wanted to look away from her, but he was helpless, tied to a horse. He could close his eyes, but that would show weakness. He kept them open. If she was going to taunt him, then she could do it to his face.

She came closer, walking with a slow undulation no doubt intended to arouse him as she purred out words in his direction. "Ye would like tae be released from yer bonds, would ye na?"

His voice rasped from dust and lack of water, but he got words out regardless. "Rather than allure me, yer soft talk is frightful enough tae raise the hairs on the back o' my neck."

Tahra walked right up and stroked his helpless body. "I canna lose this battle, nay matter what the Murrays dae. I wull obliterate yer clan. Make history completely forget ye."

Baltair made himself swallow the bile that had risen in his throat with as little production as possible.

But she'd seen it. She smirked at him, then raised her head and addressed her men. "Hang him on a tree near Murray camp, as a warning." Having dismissed everyone, she turned and went back to her trees.

The men who had brought him led the horse directly toward Murray camp.

Baltair wasn't sad, exactly. Just full of regret.

There were MacGregor cousins he had always been sure he would meet: Tavish, Tomas, and Eoin's twin Jeffrey, who called himself Friseal. Would Eoin tell them about Baltair? And about Ciaran, who would die any day now without the halberd in his hands? Perhaps even with it, because of the curse.

The only bright spot in an otherwise dark hour was his certainty that the curse would act upon Tahra, as well. Even though she was a druid child and not human. After all, the halberd took its magic from druids who had been betrayed by their own kind and entrapped inside its cursed metal.

Baltair regretted that he would never have children. How had he been so certain his children would one day know all their MacGregor cousins? Somewhere, he'd gotten the idea their whole MacGregor clan would meet every year for reunions, somewhere controlled by the clan, where they need not fear English oppression nor druid enslavement.

Most of all, he regretted stopping Ellie when she had her hands on the halberd. Not because of what was happening to him, or even to Ciaran, but because she had been right to try and stop Tahra. She had been noble and self-sacrificing, and he had scolded her for it. He regretted never telling her so.

Never apologizing. If he was going to tell her, it had to be now, before they hanged him.

At the top of his voice, Baltair yelled, "Ellie, I'm sorry I doubted ye!"

His voice echoed off the stones on top of the surrounding Highland mountains, adding to the gloom of the overcast skies.

Perhaps one day there would be peace between the Camerons and the Murrays. Someone might tell Eoin Baltair's last words. Surely Eoin would tell Ellie.

The Cameron men were talking, and now that Baltair was finished despairing, he had to hear them. He'd rather not.

"This tree be as good as any."

"Aye. 'Tis alone and beckoning."

"The Murrays wull see him hanging from afar."

They led his horse under a high branch, tied the noose around his neck, and untied him from the horse.

Instinct made him try to stall them. "Ye are na gaun'ae allow me tae sit up?"

The young Cameron who he had stared down earlier appeared, ready to oblige him.

But Teàrlach pulled the young man away by the shoulder. "He does na merit that. Ye saw the contempt with which he treated oor Tahra. A man who can treat a lady—"

Baltair spat at Teàrlach. "She is nay lady. She is na e'en a person, but a construct o' druids! Ye must remember this, if nay for my sake, then for yerselves. I say this as a brother in Christ."

"Enough o' his jawing." Teàrlach came over and whacked the horse's rear.

The horse ran. Baltair fell. The rope caught him by the neck. It hurt.

CHAPTER THIRTEEN

Hanging on as tight as she could to the horse with her legs, Ellie struggled to keep up with the men riding to rescue Baltair. This time, they didn't slow down going through the trees. The moon and stars lit them up, but the leafy ends of branches hit her in the face, nonetheless. She couldn't help flinching, but she didn't ease up.

They had to get there in time to save Baltair.

Eoin was riding up front, and it gave her hope to see him holding his hand up in the air in front of them with a shining metal object in it. She didn't know what it was, but she recognized it. He kept it in his breast pocket and always took hold of when they were about to time travel. It was a magic item from the Druids. Maybe, just maybe, it would have some protective effect on Baltair, even from a distance.

But they were going awfully fast. Wasn't he afraid of being knocked off his horse by a branch? She sure was. But she wasn't about to admit that to anyone or slow down and let them go on without her. Now that she didn't have the ring, she was back to her cowardly self. Or was she? She didn't think she was capable of rushing through the woods on horseback following after a bunch of Highlanders who, she had to admit, she'd only known for a month.

That line of thinking made her stomach queasy, and so she left it behind, instead focusing on staying on the horse and missing all the branches that were flying by. At last, the edge of the trees was in sight, not the area where Baltair had been captured. That was toward the south road. This time, they were taking a straight line over to Murray camp. It wasn't the route she'd taken with Nadia, either. The two of them had hugged the mountainside. No, this was a straight line. It would take them through the battlefield the two clans were destined to fight on tomorrow.

When Eoin broke out through the trees ahead, he spurred his horse on even faster and let out a yell that was both terrifying and heartbreaking in its intensity. As each new man broke out into the trees after him they did the same thing, so that by the time Ellie got to the clearing and was able to see out into the battlefield, she should have been prepared for what the men had almost reached. Should have.

But she wasn't. Tears broke out in her eyes and her throat choked up. Baltair was swinging by a rope around his neck from the lone tree in the middle of the battlefield. At first, she despaired that he was dead. But she soon noticed that he was moving. It hadn't broken his neck. It was a miracle.

The moonlight glinted off the object Eoin was holding aloft. Perhaps not a miracle from God, but rather magic from the Druids. She would take it. She would take and be grateful. It was her worst nightmare, seeing Baltair dead. This in the absence of her bravery ring made the battle very real for her. He was going to risk his life out the her out here tomorrow you know if you didn't lose it today.

Could she bear this the rest of her life?

Wait. Where did that thought come from?

Eoin and his men fended off the nearby Camerons while Connell rode up to the lone tree, placed Baltair on the horse behind him, and cut the rope off Baltair's neck.

Ellie urged her horse on over next to where

Baltair lay against Connell's horse. "I thought ye were dead," she blubbered through the tears that gushed from her eyes, wiping them away impatiently with the back of her hand.

His throat sounded like rocks grating against each other when he spoke, and he could barely get any noise out at all through the choking his throat still insisted on doing, even though the rope was gone. "Ye should na be here, lass. 'Tis tae dangerous for ye."

Hot prickles of rage burned her cheeks, making her get in his face. "Tae dangerous for me? Who is the one just got hanged, eh? Eh?"

Surprising her, he acquiesced by looking away and giving her the tiniest nod. And then he reached out and took hold of her saddle. "Stay steady, sae I can get on with ye, lass."

He tried to climb on in front of her.

She turned the horse slightly, putting Baltair closer to the back of the saddle than the front. "I already have my hands on the reins, ye dolt. Either ye get on behind me, or ride with Connell."

Baltair chuckled at that, making her even more angry, if that were possible. "Verra wull, verra wull. Dinna get yerself in a snit ower it. Keep yer temper doon, lass."

Torn between arguing further about just how dangerous it was for who and keeping the horse steady, Ellie found herself frustratingly quiet while he climbed on behind her.

His warmth instantly calmed her down enough to hear that the skirmish was over. Eoin and the others were waiting on them so they could leave.

Baltair couldn't just let her notice this on her own. "Ye had best turn the horse and gae, lass. I ken ye think yerself brave, but think o' me, helpless back here withoot e'en a knife. There wull be maire Camerons here soon."

Growling the whole way back through the woods to Murray camp by moonlight didn't leave much room for conversation. Ellie liked it that way. The rest of the men let her and Baltair's horse go first, so she wasn't too worried about Camerons catching up behind them. All she had to worry about was being hit off the horse by a low branch.

Baltair helped her with this, leaning this way and that with his superior weight and actually driving the horse more than she did.

She let him. The part of her that had been so stubborn and brave was thrown out with that ring. She had no idea why she'd been arguing with Baltair now. The truth was, having him behind her on the horse felt better than anything she'd ever felt in her life. She never wanted this ride to end.

All too soon, it did. They had to slow to a walk when they arrived in the camp.

Harold got up from his place at the fire and followed them over to where the horses were tied, raging at them all the while. "'Tis glad I am Baltair lives, ye ken. Howsoever, ye should na hae gone. Ye dinna ken what ye hae done. This battle is na like any ither ye hae seen. Ye hae ainly increased the chances o' some aught gang terribly wrong."

Ellie and Baltair's party dismounted and tied up their horses.

Baltair turned to face Harold. "'Twas true. They dae hae a cannon. 'Tis in Cameron camp, but if we gae in the night, mayhap we can disable it."

Harold cut Baltair off with a stubborn look to his men around him. "We hae lost oor tyme tae gae after the cannon."

Baltair put his hand on the back of Ellie's waist and walked away from Harold, toward Baltair's tent.

Harold and his men followed, with Harold pronouncing as if he sat in a throne on high, "We gae after the Cameron warriors at first light. Make your-selves ready."

When they stopped walking outside Baltair's

tent but kept arguing, Ellie turned away, fatigued, and saw Nadia's face in the crowd.

Her friend gave Ellie a look of sympathy, but Nadia's husband, Ciaran, was leaning on Nadia as if he couldn't stand without her now. And his face was deathly white. He didn't have long to live. Maybe just days.

It made Ellie realize something: she didn't care what the future consequences might be. Ellie only cared that Baltair was safe. Oh, and about Nadia, her husband, and Baltair's cousins. "Baltair," she said to him firmly, holding the tent open and gesturing inside.

When he looked up at her, he seemed grateful for a chance to walk away from Harold, which he did quickly.

CHAPTER FOURTEEN

B altair sat in his tent, listening for Raild to leave.

Ellie was smearing an especially thick poultice on the rope burns on Baltair's neck. Her face looked drawn up and disgusted. "How could they dae this tae ye? Where I hail from, no one's hanged anybody in a hundred years."

He tried not to be drawn to her eyes, but he wasn't successful. Far from disgusted, she was deeply concerned for him. She ached for his pain.

He looked away. He wanted to pull the tent open and look out to see if everyone was still hanging about, but he didn't dare draw attention to himself. Raild would never go away then.

She stopped smearing his burns. "That's as much

good as I can dae. Hope that relieves the pain a bit and helps it heal." She had drawn her hands away, but she was still looking at him with that hurt in her eyes. She didn't need to say it.

He could tell just by her bearing. She cared for him. He had tried to stop this from happening.

Finally, Raild called out to his men, "Coome, we hae preparations tae make." His tone changed, and he was addressing everyone else standing around outside Baltair's tent. "Ye all hae work as wull. As I telt ye, we gae tae face the Camerons at first light. Off with ye."

Baltair waited a few beats, then peeked out the door of his tent. When he was sure no one would notice, he pushed it farther open and—

Ellie grabbed his hand. "Ye need tae stay here and rest. Ye almost suffocated tae death. The battle's nay till morning. Ye hae tyme tae rest. Ye should take it."

He shook his hand free of her. Not unkindly, just impatiently. He didn't turn and look at her. He had already been encouraging her feelings for him. She was already too far gone as it was. Best to start inching away while he could, rather than making it worse by looking her in the eyes again.

Still, he rasped with his sore voice, "We yet need

tae disable the cannon. I hae tae get Eoin, Connell, and the others ower there tae Cameron camp tae get the job done." He got out of the tent and looked around for any of the people he wanted.

She got out of the tent too and stood next to him, helping him look. "I'm coming along."

He didn't want to argue with her in front of anyone passing by and cause her embarrassment, so he just gave her the minimum attention he could and still be polite while he walked about Murray camp, looking here and there for any of his cousins. Finally, he ended up at Ciaran's tent, talking to his nearly dead cousin.

Nadia open the door, but didn't invite them in. She simply sat back with the door open so that they could see her husband lying there, helpless to do much.

"Hae ye seen Eoin, Connell, or any of the others?" Baltair asked. "We still need tae disable that cannon I saw gang tae the Camerons. 'Tis at their camp by now, 'Twill face us on the morrow if we dinna."

Ciaran tried to sit up and talk to him.

Nadia held him down and gave him a look that said 'Och, please man, lie doon and conserve yer strength.

Ciaran gave in, ainly moving his head tae look Baltair in the eye. "Eoin, Connell, and the others man the catapult, readying it tae strike."

This steamed Baltair up. "Dinna they—"

"Searc put them tae it."

That took the wind out of Baltair's sails. He put his hands on his hips and looked from Ciaran, Nadia, and Ellie over toward the catapult and everyone he'd been counting on for help. "Wull does na Searc ken we need tae disable the cannon?"

Nadia spoke up. "He says 'tis maire important tae hae oor catapult ready. Mayhap we can dae one with the ither. Ye ken where the cannon is?"

Baltair shook his head and looked over to see if Ellie knew.

She shook her head as well, looking very disappointed in herself.

He couldn't help it, he gave her a tiny encouraging grin.

She took advantage. "I didna see where the cannon was in Cameron camp, but I did see where they were bringing it intae the camp. I ken where they likely hae put it. I hae some ideas on how we can disable it. I'm gang with Baltair, even if nay one else wull. He needs someone tae keep an eye on him, with that horrible wound tae his throat. If he

has trouble breathing, then I wull get him oot
o' there."

He should've seen this coming. It was a trap that
she'd been planning all along. He looked from Ellie
to Ciaran to Nadia, but he didn't see any help with
getting out of this. Oh well. He did what he could.
"Och. If ye are gang with me, then let us get on with
it. Tyme's a wasting." He went straight over to his
horse and climbed on.

Ellie stood right there beside him, confident that
he would bring her up with him.

He considered refusing to do so. It would be easy
to ride off without her. What was she going to do,
run after him? She wouldn't dare take someone else's
horse the night before a battle, would she?

She probably would.

He didn't dare risk it. "Here, lass. Take my hand
and come on up. But ye wull sit behind me
this time."

She giggled a little bit in his ear and then settled
in behind him, with her arms around him.

He could think of nothing else, so he was
halfway around the battlefield through the trees to
Cameron camp when he realized he had no idea how
they were going to proceed. He hated admitting that
to her, but she was already along, so he might as well

ask. "Sae what are yer ideas, about how tae disable the cannon, eh?"

"They hae their camp right up next tae the drop o' the cliff. What's tae stop us from pushing the cannon ower? I can distract them. I brought an easy and fast hot fire with me, in my pack here. I could set some tents afire. That would distract them, aye?"

"'Tis good. How long wull it take ye tae light the tents?"

"I wull ready it now, if ye slow doon a bit. I dinna want tae drop anything precious oot o' this backpack Kelsey gave me. 'Tis fancy even for my time. 'Twould be a shame tae lose any o' this."

"Verra wull." He slowed the horse to a walk and then stopped, got down, and helped Ellie down. It was best to give the horse a break anyway. He wanted to get back to Murray camp as well as over to Cameron camp tonight, after all.

They both emptied their bladders, and then he had her show him the fire she had brought. The two of them turned their backs to the camp and put the fire in front of them so they wouldn't draw attention.

He marveled at it. "'Tis an amazing thing, this high-powered lighter ye hae. Aye, 'twill dae the job."

She put the lighter, a long skinny thing, through

her belt and took out a stiff bit of folded paper, which she put in front of her eyes, then smiled.

"What hae ye got there?" he asked.

"See for yerself," she said, handing it to him.

He took it gingerly, afraid lest he damage it. He held it to his eyes and gasped. "Tis like a spyglass, but made o' paper!"

"Aye," she said. "Look all the way ower tae the left o' the camp."

He trained the machine over there. "Sure and all, the cannon rests near the cliff, as ye did say 'twould."

"Aye, and it still rests on the wagon. Easier for them tae move it. Easier for us tae ruin it."

He chuckled at her jest. "Ye hae saved me the dangerous scouting work with this machine, lass. 'Tis verra well for me, ye being along." He checked the best place to start the distraction, where they would stop and leave the horse, and the route he would take on foot to push the cannon over the cliff once she had started the fire.

Once he had shown her all this and gotten them both mounted once more, he asked her, "Are ye ready?"

She hugged his waist tight from behind him. "I'm ready for ye tae put on the speed."

He did. And having her hold onto him was even

more heavenly than him holding on to her had been, on the way from the hanging tree.

His heart sank when he saw the tents in the distance. He should have been glad. The tents were standing by themselves with no one around. It was the perfect opportunity to set the fire. But his heart sank because this meant an end to his time with her on the horse.

And then he was more angry with himself than he ever been in his life. How had he allowed her to talk him into bringing her along? She had no idea what she was doing in a battle situation. Well, she had managed to get into Tahra's tent and grab onto the halberd. He would give her that. But the guard would be up now that that it happened and...

He got ahold of himself. The fire was a good idea. It would work. He slowed the horse before they drew attention to themselves, still within the trees. They had skirted around the battlefield this time. Tomorrow was soon enough to be there.

He got down and handed her down. "I give ye the task o' starting the fire. Dae it where those tents are unguarded, there on the edge o' the camp ahead. And then run here tae the horse and ride back toward Murray camp. Their horses are tied near the cannon. I wull get one o' those and meet up with ye at the fork in the trail. Ye must leave as soon as ye hae the fire started. Dae ye hear me?"

For once, she nodded and didn't argue.

He turned to look at her quizzically in the moonlight.

She smiled and shrugged. Then whispered, "That makes sense. Ye listen when I make sense, and I listen when ye make sense. Dae we hae a deal?"

He hadn't meant to, but he kissed her again, a tender kiss full of all the longing in his heart that turned into something quite different before he gathered his wits and pulled away from her. "I could na let this gae withoot saying—"

Her eyes widened and filled with the love she had for him.

He shook his head no. "I am growing tae love ye, but that was na what I meant. There is a chance I wull be struck doon, ye ken. Ye may e'en see it happen."

She swallowed, and tears came out of her eyes as she nodded.

He fixed her with a stern look. "Ye must leave straight away, then, Ellie. Dinna put yerself in danger. If I am struck doon, ye must ride like the wind back tae Murray camp and tell them I hae been lost. Dinna coome for me..."

Tears flowed freely from her eyes now. "Aye. 'Twill be as ye say, should ye be struck doon."

"Give me tae the count o' five hundred and then gae set the tents afire, run back here, and leave. Ye wull leave."

She nodded, and then she grabbed hold of him and kissed him again, a deep aching needy kiss.

He hugged her to him for several long moments while their hearts beat together before slowly easing himself away and skulking off to find the cannon on the edge of the drop-down. The Camerons must've fancied that the safest spot, with no way to sneak up on it. Here was hoping he and Ellie proved them wrong.

CHAPTER FIFTEEN

E llie hoped Baltair was in a position where he could take advantage of her distraction and push the cannon over the cliff. She had walkie talkies in her pack, and batteries for them, but speaking into them just wouldn't work here. She had an extra smartphone and solar chargers for it and her phone. But with no cell towers, there was no way to send text messages. Never in her life had she imagined being unable to check in and see if things were going as planned.

Worry wouldn't help, though.

"...498, 499, 500."

Praying to God Baltair was ready, she crept up to the nearest Cameron tent, put the fancy PenUlt 'instaheat' lighter to it, and pulled the lighter's trigger.

The densely woven wool of the tent smoldered, but it would not catch.

She silently cursed the lighter, looking around for some kindling to light in order to get the tent hot enough. There, those leaves. She grabbed an armload of dry leaves and was about to drop them by the tent when she heard soft laughter inside and froze, thinking. Sure, this was the enemy, but they would come out as soon as they smelled smoke. She needed to find an actual empty tent.

Carrying her armload of leaves and walking slowly so as not to trip over her long skirts, she went to the next clump of tents and listened for any sounds. Relieved to hear none, she dropped her pile of leaves, shoved them all up close to the first tent with her feet, grabbed another pile of leaves and dropped them between the first tent and the second, and finally lit the first pile of leaves with her lighter.

The leaves made a lot of smoke, which would draw attention before long. Come on, leaves, make a flame hot enough to catch that blasted thick wool.

She used her skirts to fan the flames until the tent caught. Once it did, she turned and ran for her horse. Before she got to it, she heard alarmed voices behind her.

"What the devil is gang on here?"

"That tent has caught fire!"

"Push it doon!"

"That next tent has caught fire as wull!"

"Someone did this with purpose!"

"There she is! Get her!"

Ellie had made it to her horse, but she was shaking all over. She grabbed the saddle and went to mount, but her foot missed the stirrup.

She heard several people running toward her.

Her heart galloped in her chest.

Angry at herself for being so afraid she was useless, she roared to give herself strength. This time, her foot went into the stirrup. She mounted and rode for all she was worth, hearing the frustrated cries of those behind her.

"She is getting away!"

"Dinna stand aboot. Gae and get a horse!"

By now, Ellie was used to the branches hitting her face as she rode by. Used to the fear of being knocked off by a low hanging branch. What she couldn't take was the fear in her heart that Baltair wouldn't meet her at the fork in the trail. He had prepared her for seeing him struck down, but what if he just wasn't there at the rendezvous? How long should she wait for him? Another count of 500? No, more like 5,000, right?

Ellie ducked under an especially low-lying branch but didn't rein the horse in. "Gae on back toward yer herd, boy. Gae quick as ye can." She drew close to the fork in the trail. She could see it up ahead.

He wasn't there. Just a little further now, and then what?

The strength that came to her now was feigned, an act. It had come often when her parents were fighting and ignoring her, at best. At worst, they had forgotten to pick her up at school.

In fifth grade, Ellie had taken the magazine drive seriously, going to every neighbor's house on her street by herself and asking if they would buy a magazine subscription to support her school. Three did. Out of ten. Ellie had considered that good, until...

* * *

Mrs. McKenzie, the last neighbor on Ellie's street, made Ellie work for it. She listened politely, invited Ellie in for tea and cookies, and then suggested improvements in the way Ellie sold the magazines.

Ellie looked at her with uncertainty. "Should I give you my improved sales pitch now?"

Mrs. McKenzie smiled, got up from the dining room table, and shook her head no. "Oh no, my dear. You should come back tomorrow on a new visit and give me your improved pitch. And I suggest you wait until after that to try and sell to any more of the neighbors. Remember, you must figure out about each neighbor which magazine would appeal to them and then sell them on that. It will be much more effective than if you just appeal to them to support your school, trust me."

Ellie would've loved to ask her parents for their advice on this, but as usual when she got home, they were yelling at each other about stupid stuff. Whether the dishwasher should be loaded with the dishes facing up or down. How often the sheets should be changed. Why couldn't they wake up and notice that she needed them?

So she went to her room in front of her mirror and practiced what Mrs. McKenzie had told her. It made sense. She also went online and researched her neighbor's hobbies. Social media made this quite easy.

The next day, she went to see her neighbor right off the school bus and started the script they had prepared together. "Hello, Mrs. McKenzie."

"Why hello, Ellie. Would you like to come in?"

"Why yes, thank you." Was it time, now? She looked into her neighbor's eyes for confirmation.

Mrs. McKenzie smiled and nodded yes.

So Ellie went into her new and improved sales pitch. "I notice you like to grow rhododendrons in the front yard, and it so happens that I am selling a subscription to Gardening Magazine. It has many good hints about what might work that you won't find online. The magazine's advertisers like to hold a bit back from what's available to everyone so that they can get subscribers. Your rhododendrons would be better than anyone else's in town."

Mrs. McKenzie smiled at her and got her purse. "Why, I do believe I would like a subscription to Gardening Magazine, Ellie. Who should I make the check to, and for how much?"

Buoyed by her new confidence in how to sell magazine subscriptions, in the next two weeks, Ellie visited every house in the subdivision, venturing farther from home until she had 212 magazine subscriptions on the day they were due.

As she left for school the next Friday, she

reminded Mom, "You're picking me up from school today, right? I have that meeting after school, where they'll announce the winners of the magazine drive, so I won't be able to take the school bus."

"Oh don't worry," Mom said. "I'll pick you up at 4 o'clock. Now hurry, or you'll miss the school bus."

Reassured that her mother had heard her for once, Ellie gave her a kiss and rushed out the door.

The whole school day was unbearably boring, but finally the after school meeting came. Ellie had to sit through the fourth place winner, the third place winner, and the second place winner. Finally, they announced the winner of the magazine drive. "And first place, which includes this handcrafted replica of our school, goes to Ellie! Congratulations, Ellie. You did a great job."

Ellie had never felt more proud. She knew she had earned this. Other kids' parents had sold the magazine subscriptions for them at work, but she had done all the work herself. She marched up and put her arms out for the replica, then turned around and showed it to her competitors proudly as she walked back to her seat. The thing was a bit cumbersome, but it wasn't too heavy for her to carry.

She took the replica out to the front of the school

and texted her mom. "Okay, I'm ready for you to pick me up. I won the magazine drive!"

For the first few minutes waiting for a text back, Ellie smiled and waved at the other kids as they left the magazine drive meeting. Several of them stopped to admire her model of the school.

But after a quarter hour had passed, dread began to take hold. Mom still hadn't answered the text. Ellie called. Straight to voicemail. She called Dad. Straight to voicemail. Her parents had moved her away from family for Dad's job, clear across the country from her grandmother and her aunt and uncle. There was no one else she trusted enough to ask for a ride home from school.

Might as well get it over with, she told herself. The good news was most of the other kids had already left. Only a few stragglers walked by.

She lifted up the model of the school and rested it on her waist as best she could, but it became more and more cumbersome. In order to keep hold of it, she had put her arms out awkwardly to the sides and hug the thing to her.

Ellie walked the 5 miles home with her head held high, as if she walked that far every day with a big bulky cumbersome thing to carry.

* * *

BOTH ELLIE AND THE HORSE PANTED FOR BREATH when she stopped him, fighting tears at not finding Baltair here at the fork in the trail, where he had promised he would be. She would wait just a moment in case he was on his way and just a bit behind schedule, and then she would move out of sight—

She heard hoofbeats. Was it Baltair, or was it the Camerons coming to find her? Best move out of the trail, just in case.

She was halfway into the trees when she heard his voice. "Gae on, Ellie! 'Tis done! Gae!" It was him. It was Baltair.

Full of relief and exultation, she turned back onto the trail just in time to ride beside him back to Murray camp. "We did it!"

He reached out and hugged her sideways as they both sat their horses. "Aye, we did it. Yer fire was brilliant. It worked a charm. 'Twas the perfect plan ye had, and I could na hae done it withoot ye. Nor would I hae wanted tae." He almost kissed her as well, but visibly stopped himself, looking at her with two kinds of urgency at once. Her safety won out.

"We need tae get back tae camp, lest they send oot scouts who wull catch us."

She nodded her agreement with her face still inches from his. "Aye, we dae."

With the promise of kisses to come in his bright excited eyes, he patted her leg and then waved her on to precede him. "I wull ride behind ye. If they dae send scouts, they wull hae tae get through me tae get tae ye."

She gave him a triumphant smile, which he returned, and then rode on ahead, reassured to hear the beats of his horse's hoofs behind her.

But their victory was quickly ruined when they saw Murray camp in a panicked rush to prepare for battle. The catapult was manned with one of the twelve-person teams who had drilled on it. Nearly everyone else was mounted. All the tents had been struck, and the warriors were forming up with weapons in hand.

Ellie followed Baltair over to Eoin and Connell.

Eoin gave them a face that said both 'Where hae ye been?' and 'Look oot, Harold's after ye.'

Nadia and Ciaran were nearby on Ciaran's horse. Nadia was in front, and she had Ciaran tied to her. The man was barely there, he was so pale and sickly.

Connell said to Baltair, "Ye woke the enemy early. The watch hae already seen the Camerons approaching, na far behind ye."

Now that he said so, Ellie could hear the Camerons coming.

Baltair gave Ellie a quick kiss that only whet her appetite for more, much more. "Gae on with Eoin, now, he said, riding over next to Connell.

She looked after Baltair with puzzlement for a moment before she realized of course she couldn't go with him into battle.

Eoin beckoned to Ellie. "I'm taking ye, Nadia, and Ciaran back tae Celtic University."

No.

She wasn't leaving.

Ellie rode over next to Nadia instead.

Clinging to her cursed husband's leg with one hand and her reins with the other, Nadia turned away from Eoin and looked at Ellie with a question in her eyes, and just the tiniest spark of hope.

Peering into her friend's worried face with her own insistent face, Ellie urged Nadia, "I will na let Baltair and his cousins die in a battle they canna win, nor let yer husband die for lack o' the attempt. We need tae fight the halberd's magic with magic o' oor ain." She watched Nadia's face for any signs of agreement.

The light came back into her friend's eyes, and she nodded ever the slightest.

Encouraged, Ellie pressed on. "I believe the part in Harold's book aboot the fae is true. We must needs gae tae them. Let us get magic o' oor ain."

Nadia and Ciaran both got the same weird look on their faces and nodded yes. "Aye," said Nadia. "'Tis the ainly way we can help. Let us gae."

Before Eoin could grab them and take them back to their time, the three rode off up the mountain toward where Harold's book said the faeries lived.

CHAPTER SIXTEEN

Baltair and Connell stuck close to Eoin while Searc led them into battle against the Camerons. Instead of fighting on the battlefield, they fought on horseback amid the trees. The Camerons had obviously planned this attack, but for the Murrays and MacEacharnas, it was a brutal and bloody skirmish, rather than a proper battle. The Camerons came from the side of the trail in small packs, popping out of the trees to get them. A volley of arrows had taken down several Murrays and MacEacharnas before the mounted warriors arrived, armed with pikes.

From the front, where he rode with Raild, Searc turned back toward them and urged, "Stay close taegither. Dinna let them divide ye."

For a while, they were able to follow this order.

Baltair stuck his pike into Dougal, injuring the Cameron's shoulder so that he gave up the fight. Next he fought Ian, clanging pikes with the man while jockeying about in the woods until he was able to stick the Cameron in the leg and chase him off. Next it was Dougal's brother, Brian, who got stabbed in the gut and would surely die.

There was no taunting nor teasing this time. Not from either side. There were only thrusts and blocks and jabs, breathlessly carried out and received. Every movement mattered when it might be a person's last.

Baltair didn't fight for revenge on those who had wronged him. He didn't fight out of anger or greed or any sense of honor. He fought for his life.

He had many more such fights and was growing tired.

Eoin's voice came from his left. "Where are they getting fresh fighters from?"

Connell answered him. "They hae divided themselves up intae small factions who attack and retreat verra quickly in a circular motion. 'Tis modern warfare."

Eoin fought off his current Cameron attacker, then yelled, "We need tae dae the same!"

Searc was far ahead of them in the forest, so he didn't hear this, but he was a seasoned warrior and leader of warriors. Baltair felt confident Searc would do right by the men.

Baltair's new attacker was indeed fresh and rested. Baltair held his own, avoiding injury, but he no longer had the stamina to drive the man back. His breath came in quick puffs as he jockeyed for position, doing his best to keep the attacker in front of him and the horse, where they presented the smallest target.

"Retreat!" came the command from Searc. "Fall back tae the stones!" This meant to the catapult, whose ammunition of hundreds of stones provided shelter, as well. It had been agreed not to say the word 'catapult.' The Camerons might know of it from their spies, but why tip the Murray hand if not?

More relieved that he cared to admit, Baltair made one last jab with his pike before he turned his horse and urged it to run away, only to be shocked by a flight of arrows that thankfully went over his and his cousins' heads.

"Enough o' this," Baltair called out to Eoin. "We need tae use the stones tae break up that squad o' archers. Let us gae and tell the crew."

Eoin nodded and joined him and Connell, plus a

few of their friends, on the trail back to Murray camp. They were near the rear of the whole clan, so they were now in the front of the retreat.

The team manning the catapult looked surprised to see them, but they were already busy carrying and loading stones, even firing them.

Thankful that hundreds of stones had been gathered, Baltair asked the catapult crew, "Where are ye firing, men? We hae na seen the effects at all, oot there i' the fight."

Sean Murray looked up at Baltair as he carried his stone up to the catapult and loaded it with a grunt. "Raild telt us tae fire at the center o' the battlefield, where most o' their forces should be concentratit."

Baltair cursed violently, making his horse stamp. "Nay, they are fighting us in the trees on the trail tae the battlefield. We need ye tae take oot their archers." He dismounted and went to the small map that had been drawn of the area and used charcoal to make X marks on it. "They hae archers stationed here and here. There will na be any o' oor men there. We hae retreated. Besides, we canna get close enough tae take anyone oot, the archers are sae good."

Sean shook his head no with his eyes full of apology. "I canna change orders for ye, Baltair. Ainly for Searc, or mayhap Raild."

Baltair had known this would be true, but he had given it a try out of desperation. He remounted and turned his horse back toward the fighting. "Wull their writ be enough, or must ye hear their word?"

"Their writ wull be enough. Godspeed."

Getting to Searc was ten times harder than fighting the Camerons' sideward attack on the trail had been. Their clan's war chief had been at the front and was only in the rear because the clan was retreating.

Their own warriors passed them by, tightly packed on the trail. Baltair and his cousins and friends had to go against the stream, while at the same time telling everyone else, "Nay, dinna follow us. Ye still need tae retreat."

Baltair asked Gordon Murray, "Hae ye seen Searc? How far yet?"

Gordon looked a bit worried when he answered, "Aye, Searc is na far."

Connell had heard this, because he rode faster, keeping to the trail but more on the left edge of it. Eoin, Baltair, and the others followed.

When they rounded the bend of the trail and saw Searc and Raild, Baltair understood Gordon's worry. The two leaders were working hard to keep the Camerons off the rear of the main party, and they were just about out of stamina.

"Yah!" Connell called out, urging his horse into a gallop.

Baltair heard Eoin and their other friends do the same to the right of him. In moments, Connell was in the fight, as were Eoin and the others. Baltair held his sword up to fend off any comers, but he concentrated on telling Searc, "Ye hae tae get the archers. Ye canna get the battlefield." He dared not say more, lest the catapult still be a secret, and he give it away.

Searc got a gleam in his eye and gave Baltair a seated bow of thanks as he galloped away. Raild stayed to help guard the rear a few moments so that Searc had a chance to get back to Murray camp — what was left of it— and the catapult to stop the archers.

The fighting was brutal, but the short respite Baltair and his group had made them the fresh soldiers this time. The Camerons were the weary ones now. They drove the Camerons back for three turns of the battle.

Eoin nodded to Baltair, who nodded to the next man, who nodded to the next, until the last man was nodding at Eoin. As one, they all turned to retreat together. It was a move they had long been drilling, on days the clan didn't have a battle.

Even still, it was a close escape, but God smiled on the Murrays. The long-clear sky had clouded at last, and now it opened up. A torrent of Scottish rain poured down.

Baltair said a silent prayer of thanks. He'd been positive fiery arrows would come next. He smiled. Even God knew an ounce of prevention was worth a pound of cure.

CHAPTER SEVENTEEN

E llie let the horse pick its way up the mountain, awed by how good the steed was at the job. She supposed she shouldn't have been, but there was no way any vehicle she had ever driven would make it up here.

"There be some aught tae say, aboot livestock," she said to Nadia when the two horses brought them close enough to speak.

Nadia's face was gaunt with worry about Ciaran, but she managed a small smile of agreement. "Aye, there be much tae say aboot this time. 'Tis simpler. Closer tae Nature."

Ellie was ready to argue about it being a more brutal time, and what was Nadia thinking. But she knew what Nadia was thinking, and she wasn't going to add to the woman's grief. Let Nadia make light of the situation.

Normally, that was Ellie's role, albeit through jokes. That aggression ring had changed her. She saw now that the ring had made her far too reckless. But the bravery it brought out? It had been in her all along. She'd been making light of situations ever since her parents' death. She should have been facing problems head on. She had what it took. She hoped that from now on she would use that and do what she ought. Making everyone laugh was fun for the moment, but doing the right thing helped you sleep at night.

The way up the mountain was treacherous and slow. Five times they stopped for water and rest, both for themselves and for the horses. It was too difficult to get Ciaran on his feet, but Ellie and Nadia got down to lessen their burdens. They let the horses drink from the mountain streams they found — not an easy thing, that. More often than not, the water came out of a small cave in the mountain and only was visible briefly before going back underground.

"Snowmelt," Nadia said once when Ellie was staring at the water, wondering where it came from.

Ellie laughed a bit. "Och, aye. Some aught sae simple as melted snow never occurs tae me. We are tae spoilt, in the modern world. Tae far removed."

Nadia paused from giving Ciaran a drink and smiled at Ellie. "Are ye gaun'ae miss the modern world?"

"Whatever dae ye mean?"

"Ye canna fool me. Ye are gaun'ae stay with Baltair, here in his time."

Tears sprang to Ellie's eyes. "I am if he lives through this battle." She looked around. "We dinna ken where Harold's faerieland is, ainly that 'tis up this mountain. We hae coome far enough. I'm gaun'ae ask the fae now, for their aid."

A circle of trees around the mountain a bit caught Ellie's eye. Leaving her horse there to graze on the short but deep green mountain grass, she made her way there on foot, with tears falling from her eyes faster than she could wipe them away.

"Ellie!" Nadia called after her. "Ellie, wait!"

Ellie wasn't going to wait. She had waited long enough. The faeries could hear them anywhere. Why did they have to go someplace special to talk to them? "We hae gone far enough away that the battle will na get us. ''Tis all we need."

"But Ellie, faeries dinna deal lightly. In all the tales, they ask far more than anyone would want tae give. Mayhap we should leave the fae oot o' it and let things unfold."

Poor Nadia. She was accepting Ciaran's imminent death. She had lost hope.

Ellie told her, "Ye can let things unfold as they wull if ye want, Nadia. I wull na hold it agin ye. Howsoever, I am dang this. I wull na let the Murray clan lose, if I hae some aught tae dae aboot it. The warriors are trying sae hard. And Baltair..." Tears flooded down her face. Sobs choked her throat so bad, she fell down on the ground and wiped her tears off the moss that grew on the roots of this circle of trees.

Ellie thrashed and cried and sobbed and called out to the faeries until she was exhausted and collapsed in a heap of weeping. "Dae ye hear me, faeries? I give ye my tears in exchange for help with the battle below. Help the Murrays and MacEacharnas win the fight and keep their lands. The Camerons hae the druids on their side, use o' the druid halberd. Nadia says the fae hae tasted the halberd's power. Fae power is stronger than druid power, ye ken?"

She heard nothing. No answer. Not even an indication they heard her. Maybe faeries weren't real after all.

Nadia was next to her on the ground, crying too, and soaking the ground with her own tears. And wonder of wonders, Ciaran was there as well. All three of them cried all the tears they had, soaking the ground, until the sun set and they all fell asleep cuddled together for warmth, there on the moss.

Before sleep overtook her, Ellie was able to ask Nadia, "Did ye hobble the horses?"

"Aye."

* * *

LAUGHTER FILLED THE FOREST. THE LAUGHTER of someone behind you, laughing at you. Every time Ellie turned to see who it was, she saw only trees. The light was in between sunlight and moonlight. It wasn't starlight, more like candlelight. Oh! Out of the corner of her eye, she saw a million lights. Fireflies, that's what they were. The forest was full of fireflies, swirling in the air at great speed and laughing.

* * *

Ellie didn't want to wake up, but her bladder was full. What time was it? She would run to the bathroom and then go put the kettle on and have a nice hot cup of tea. She had preferred coffee at home in the states, but ever since she started working at Celtic University, the tea they drank here in Scotland was growing on her.

When Ellie opened her eyes, she was greeted with forest all around her.

What the heck?

Seeing Nadia's sleeping face reminded her where she was, what was going on. The dried tear stains running down her friend's face broke her heart.

What about Ciaran? Was he still breathing?

A rush of fear overtook Ellie. She got up and checked on Nadia's husband. As she did so, something heavy dragged on her sleeve as it fell off her arm. What was it? She looked down.

There in the green moss lay an intricately made silver axe. Slender and delicate, it was the length of her arm, but the handle was only the width of her finger. At the joint of the handle and the blade was a silver metal flower. Inside the flower was a shining amber stone the shape of a firefly.

Something niggled at the back of Ellie's mind. Something she wanted to know. What was it? Her eyes wandered around aimlessly until they landed on Ciaran.

As if a mist shunted out of her mind, it was finally clear. Oh, right. She rushed over to Ciaran and put her hand on his neck to see if his heart was still beating.

It was, but weakly.

Ciaran looked more pale than ever as he opened his eyes. "The faerie axe!" he said with a breathy voice, then paused to rest a moment before breathing out his next words. "Where did ye get it?"

She hadn't realized she'd picked it up until he said that. She raised it between them so they could both examine it. "Just like the one in the book, aye?"

He nodded where he lay, eyes half open, face contorted in pain. "Has it the same powers, dae ye ken?"

Nadia had woken up now too and was sitting up in earnest, eyes fixed on the silver weapon with the glowing amber stone. "In the event there be any chance it does hae the same powers as the axe in the book, ye need tae get it doon tae the battle."

Ellie nodded as she backed away from them

toward where the horses were hobbled. "Ye could dae worse than tae bide here. 'Tis safe, sae far."

Nadia put her arms around her husband and nodded to Ellie. "God be with ye."

CHAPTER EIGHTEEN

What used to be Murray camp was dark now, but rest was nowhere to be had. Life was just lifting one stone after another and carrying it to the catapult carefully, so as not to slip in the mud, while watching the rest of the clan fight off one Cameron after another, with no end in sight.

Baltair kept directing the stones to be carried over to the catapult, taking his own turn at carrying when it came up and cursing the rain all the while, for making the ground so slick. He had drilled this with the men, and they were efficient. But not in mud.

Cameron warriors kept coming despite it all, roaring and swinging swords and pikes, and overall ready for battle. Even though the Murrays had thrown three quarters of their stones. Even though the rain still beat down on them. Even though it was past dark and the former Murray camp was littered with fallen warriors whose bones cracked under the trampling feet of horse after horse.

Eoin's voice caught Baltair's attention from across the camp, calling out in pain.

Baltair held his hand over his eyes to catch the rain from clouding his vision, searching for his cousin. There. Oh, he yet lived. Still mounted, Eoin was riding toward Baltair, holding his left arm. Blood soaked his left sleeve.

Baltair ran up and tied his belt around Eoin's arm above the wound to stop the bleeding. Some people called this by its French name, a tourniquet. The Scots just called it using one's brains to stay alive.

Once it was tied, Eoin was all business again, raising his sword and going to the front to continue fighting the Camerons off the catapult.

The catapult team were down to a quarter of their original stone supply, and the Murray side had lost more men than the Cameron side had, by far. Baltair eyed the stones again, and looked around the surrounding area to see if there any more they might use. There were not, of course. They had gathered them already, in the weeks leading up to this fight.

The book Nadia had stolen from Tahra had warned them in plenty of time, that the battle was coming. They had built the catapult, confident it would give them the edge they needed to beat the advantage they had lost, when Tahra somehow had managed to get Raild's manuscript.

Baltair cursed, then watched Searc until the war chief looked his way and met his eyes.

With his weary but determined face dripping rain water, the Murray war chief swallowed and looked to the other men, just as Baltair had done, gauging how many they had left. Would Searc choose to fight this battle to the death of all, Baltair wondered, or would he surrender soon in order to save a few? The children and the non-fighting women of course had been sent off to safety before the battle started. Some were at Murray castle. But this branch of them would come to an end, if the battle was allowed to play out. Tahra had bewitched too many allies into joining the Cameron side.

Baltair looked over to Raild, to see if he was near the same determination.

Oddly, the old time traveler in his younger self's body was not considering surrender. He kept looking up the mountain with hope in his eyes. What could he possibly hope to get? The man couldn't truly believe the fae would come to their aid. Certies, the man had written a tall tale about just that, but how could any grown man depend on such flights of fancy?

One of the Camerons had fought his way through the Murray defense. He had lost his horse while getting through, but he was coming near the catapult on foot, sword in hand and scowl on rain-soaked face.

Baltair tossed the stone he'd been carrying at the man's feet, missed, drew his sword, and met the man in a fight. He had been fighting for eight hours, and yet he still found the strength to raise his sword when needed. Clang, clang, clang. Strike, parry, move. Baltair gave it all he had, each and every time.

Eoin rode over and finished Baltair's attacker with a grand slice of his sword, breaking the man in twain at the waist, then returned to the battle front.

Grateful, Baltair turned back to his task of loading the catapult. The forest was thick, and the catapult was taking out the Cameron forces still on the trail to get to where the Murray camp had been. The more they could take out before they got here, the better. The men were loading and firing and loading and firing as fast as they could, but they had been at this for hours. They were slowing down. And running out of stones.

Raild was looking up at the mountain, and his face lightened with joy.

Baltair looked up to see what the man was gawking at and stopped dead in his tracks. "Ellie! Gae back! Save yerself!" he yelled as fervently as he could, waving his arms in the air toward the mountain.

She kept coming as if she hadn't heard him. Now he saw she had something in her hands, a weapon.

Completely made of silver and resembling the most graceful branch of a spring-flowering tree, it drew his full attention, shining in the sunlight —but it was night. Where was the light coming from? The stars and moon weren't bright enough. The wonder which had bloomed in his mind and heart at the sight of the weapon blossomed into full flower.

The light emanated from the weapon, itself. It was a blue light, like that of the hottest parts of a fire. But it wasn't burning Ellie's hands. She held it like she would a twig.

This was the fae axe. The one Ciaran wielded in Raild's book. The one that had made Ciaran a conqueror in that book, though the book made no mention of any druid child. The fae axe glowed with power all its own, pulsated with it.

What was Ellie doing with the faerie axe? It magnified the abilities, natural or otherwise, of the bearer. Ellie had some fighting ability because he'd been teaching her, but hardly any at all compared to anyone else here. Even with the magnification, she would be helpless if she tried to fight with it.

More frantic than ever, Baltair ran toward Ellie's horse even as she rode toward him. "Ellie, ye must give it tae me. Dinna try tae use it yerself. Hand it doon!" He extended his hand out to receive the thing.

Would she give it to him? Was it like the halberd which had ruined Ciaran? Was it bewitching her and cursing her strength even now, before she used it? He had to get it away from her, even if it was the last thing he did.

Out of the corners of his eyes, Baltair was aware that one by one, every man in the area had turned to face Ellie. Even the Camerons. In just a few moments, the battle had stopped and everyone was still. Staring.

Ellie met Baltair's eyes as she rode over to him. She stopped her horse, and it stood blowing air out of its nose while she leaned down and handed him the exquisite silver axe. As soon as she had, she turned the horse and rode away at a walk.

Baltair felt all alone, even though Ellie was back and he was surrounded by the Murrays and the MacEacharnas. Standing or mounted, they were all deathly still, transfixed by the fae axe.

He was, too. It made him feel taller than a giant, stronger than a bull, and faster than the wind. He stood staring at it till he heard everyone murmuring around him.

"Tahra is here."

CHAPTER NINETEEN

The Druid child had the halberd in her hands. Surrounded by the rain-washed land and her exhausted brainwashed men, she stood dry as the inside of a stove. She wore her white robes, and there were flowers in her long golden hair.

As if transfixed, everyone backed up, leaving the two magical foes to face each other in a circle of faces.

Tahra smiled as if she had been responsible for this somehow and it pleased her.

Enough of this. Baltair raised the enchanted weapon in front of him and willed it to smite her down.

A huge see-through fist arose up out of the faerie axe. It was as big as a cloud and almost as high. With a whooshing sound, it slammed down to pound the druid child into the ground whence she came.

The crowd stood dumbfounded with their jaws hanging open and their eyes round. They didn't move, just stood there watching, spellbound. Even the horses were quiet. But as the fist came down, they all backed away with silent footsteps.

Tahra held the halberd up over her head, cocked back. When the fist came down, she swung the halberd forward.

Baltair laughed at the druid child in his mind. She looked ever so much the child, just now, with her fists raised against someone much larger and stronger. About to be taught a lesson.

But his laugh was cut short. The halberd sliced the fist clean in half. The two sides fell away and dissolved into a cold mist that chilled Baltair to the bone, making him shiver.

Tahra was left standing. Unharmed and apparently unaffected by the mist, she turned her evil gaze on Baltair. Lightning split the stormy night sky. The only lightning they'd seen had been a few days ago. This wasn't a thunderstorm, but the druid child and the halberd were turning it into one.

The lightning crackled and sizzled, gathering

strength, until one giant blaze struck straight down at Baltair.

He didn't tell the faerie axe what to do, only held it up in front of him and willed it to protect him. The precise phrase he used when thinking toward it was, "Help!"

And it did help him. While still making him feel taller than a giant, stronger than a bull, and faster than the wind, it formed a bubble around him, clear as glass and just as soundproof.

None of the noise of the lightning reached him here. He could no longer hear the horses breathing or the rain falling.

And och! Raindrops were stopped by an unseen smooth surface half his arm's length away from his face above his head. Each new drop pooled there briefly before running down around the sides of the bubble and dripping off it in a circle around where he stood, now perfectly dry.

A blink of the eye later, lightning struck the puddle the rain had made on the sides of his bubble.

He felt nothing. Heard nothing. The smell, though. The inside of the bubble smelled like ashes in the fireplace, only stronger.

Thrice more the lightning struck at him, and thrice more the bubble stopped it.

Tahra's face got more and more determined as she bade the halberd throw lightning bolt after lightning bolt at Baltair's glass bubble. Apparently without her knowledge, her feet took her closer and closer to him, one jerky step at a time. With the halberd thrown back over her right shoulder in a menacing manner. It was only a matter of time before she got close enough to swing the halberd into his bubble.

Would his little silver axe strengthen the glass so the halberd couldn't break it?

And how much energy did she have left within her person, to fuel the halberd's magic? Ciaran said the foul druid implement drained energy from him whenever he used its magic, and that the same effects had been seen on Tahra the last time he saw her wield the cursed weapon that had drained Ciaran for good, not allowing him to heal from druid magic which should have restored him to full health.

All this lightning had to be taking its toll on Tahra. Perhaps she was more crafty than Baltair gave her credit for. Was she approaching on purpose and only feigning the jerky movement of her legs? Was her magic power running out? Did she have the halberd cocked back deliberately to strike at the bubble?

He had to assume that was the case. He didn't feel the fae draining his own strength through their axe. Quite the contrary, he still felt strong as a bull here in his bubble, dry amid the rain and unaffected amid the lightning strikes.

However, Tahra's mean-spirited eyes left their determined focus on him and searched for another target. Their gaze wandered over his shoulder and landed on something behind him. They squinted evilly at the corners, seeming to turn up the edges of her mouth in a wicked grin as she considered whatever it was behind him that had caught her attention. Subtly, in a movement only a warrior would notice, she tilted the halberd, aiming it over his shoulder in his stead.

For a moment, Baltair could not imagine what had distracted her. What would she possibly want to kill more than him, the one who had the faerie axe which had almost crushed her?

His brain found the answer and told his body before it told his mind. His body reacted. A chill came over him. At the same time, battle heat rose in his chest, strengthening his arms even beyond what the faerie axe had done.

All this happened within Baltair because Tahra

was looking at Ellie. Ellie was the druid child's new target. Defenseless Ellie.

Lightning no longer struck Baltair's bubble,. It roiled in the sky as it had before the druid child told it to strike him. Flashes would come out from the side and grow across the sky as the small overhead storm whirled chains of light in the air high above them, lighting up the night sky as if it were day in more and more frequent bursts of white-hot energy.

Baltair hadn't seen lightning strike anything.

Before she died, Searc's mother told him about a time she saw lightning strike a tree. Searc told the rest of them. The top of the tree looked fine afterward, but from the point where it was struck to deep down into the earth, including the roots, the tree was black and lifeless. It never recovered. It took years, but gradually the part above the blackened trunk and roots faded away and fell off. There was nothing left of that tree now, twenty years later.

Just as Baltair's body was aware of the peril before his mind was, his feet started running toward Tahra before his mind caught hold of just what danger Ellie was in. If he could get to Tahra and knock her over, that would stop her attack on Ellie. It had to. Aye, destroying the druid child's concentration would break the spell the halberd had on the lightning.

Baltair made his feet run faster than they ever had. He didn't have to cover much ground. Only 20 paces. It was the longest 20 paces he had ever run.

The bubble ran with him, keeping him dry and protected.

"Never mind me, protect Ellie!" he yelled, and the sound reverberated inside his throat, ears, and head, but not anywhere else. It never made it outside the bubble.

Tahra had understood him, though. Her beautiful face was still contorted into an ugly mask of malevolence, but there was now an amused look in her eyes. She directed the halberd over toward Ellie as if she were throwing something. And she was. She was throwing the lightning.

He was almost on her. He just had to jump into her and knock her over and he would stop the lightning attack. He would save Ellie's life.

He jumped.

Before he knocked her over —which he did— he heard the lightning strike behind him. His heart sank even as he landed on top of the druid child, swung the faerie axe, and chopped off her head.

Tahra's dead hand dropped the halberd onto the wet grass.

The halberd lay there, trying to look innocent and be forgotten, as if all this could have happened without its magic.

Baltair knew better. Rage soared through him as, raising the axe over his head just as Tahra had raised her weapon, he lowered it down and struck the halberd, first on its handle and then on its blade.

This made no sense. Silver was much softer than iron. The axe should have been demolished, while the stalwart iron halberd should yet lie there, unaffected.

But there was magic.

Glowing with faerie fire, the silver axe went through the iron of the halberd like a hot knife through butter—handle, blade, and all. Baltair chopped the halberd into wee bits.

With his rage slowly ebbing into sorrow, he turned to go over to Ellie's poor lightning-struck body and see if her knapsack had survived. He would get the lighter she had shown him, and burn the remaining parts of the wooden handle of the halberd.

He had stormed halfway over to Ellie before he realized she was still mounted on her horse.

Very much alive, she was staring down at the ground in horror.

Baltair followed her gaze down to the ground as he climbed up on her horse and clung to her.

Someone lay there. Black from the lightning strike, the body was unrecognizable.

The warriors were waking up as if from a standing sleep, shaking their heads and rubbing their eyes. All of the Camerons looked uncertain, and who could blame them? No longer behind the magic druid child, they had no idea why they were here or what was going on. Baltair wouldn't be surprised if all their minds had been addled the entire time and the whole fight had been her idea and not theirs at all.

Connell sat his horse nearby.

Baltair asked him, "Who is it? Who took the lightning bolt for Ellie?"

But Ellie was the one who answered him, her voice soft and disbelieving. "Harold jumped in front o' the lightning for me. He gave his life sae that I could live. He would na even look at me when I looked at him, but he gave his life for me. The faeries hae their sacrifice."

Ciaran's voice came from the mountain now, clear and strong, startling Baltair so that he almost fell down. "It could hae been ye, Ellie. We were sae afeared it would be ye that we came rushing doon the mountain tae stop ye. The bravery ye hae is sae verra good and true. I wull be delighted tae call ye cousin."

By the time Baltair looked up the mountain, saw Nadia and Ciaran up there on horseback, and told Connell, the man had already seen it for himself and was on his way. Baltair signaled Eoin. The whole MacGregor faction met up, dismounted, and clumped into a family hug with whoops and hollers and rejoicing.

Amid it all, Baltair stood next to Ellie with his arm around her, soaking in her closeness.

CHAPTER TWENTY

D uring a lull in the conversation, Eoin beckoned them all close. "In Harold's book, Ciaran uses the faerie axe tae travel distance as wull as through time. Let us try it oot, shall we?" He looked over at his brother Connell. "Would na ye love tae gae and see Mither and Da? How long has it been syne we were all taegither?"

Connell raised his eyebrows and looked to the rest of them, knowing they had all read the book except him. "It has been auld lang syne. I would love tae gae see them. Could na we get oor brothers Jeffrey and Meehall as wull?"

"Dinna forget Meehall's wife Sarah," said Ciaran enthusiastically.

Connell looked pleased to hear this. "Upon what dae we wait?" he asked everyone.

Ciaran smiled at him. "For one, I dinna think we wull need horses there."

They rode down and returned their horses to the Murrays for safekeeping, tying them to the tie line with the rest of the herd.

Searc came up and clapped an arm around Baltair's shoulders. "Ye did a fine job manning the catapult and keeping the crew running, Baltair."

Ellie knew that recognition from the war chief for his fighting abilities and leadership was important to Baltair. She expected him to break out in a huge smile.

Baltair, however, played it down, simply clasping forearms with Searc nonchalantly. "'Tis an honor tae serve ye in any capacity, Searc." He looked around at them all. "We're gaun'ae visit the rest o' our clan. I dinna ken when we wull return tae ye."

Searc looked from Baltair to Ciaran to Eoin and finally landed on Connell, whom he gave a polite nod before reaching out and clasping forearms. "Ye are all welcome tae return and live with us. I am also honored tae fight beside ye."

Ellie thought Searc gave her an extra look, and then she was sure of it when he gave her a wink. It brought the red to her cheeks, she could feel it. Things were still uncertain between her and Baltair.

Eoin took the lead again, and this time Ellie didn't mind letting him. That ring really had been a big influence on her. "Let's walk up the mountain a ways. They ken we hae the faerie axe and it can dae magic, but the less talk there is aboot us, the better."

There was a general nod of agreement, and they all followed him up the mountain. They were now out of sight, but they could look down and see the former camp. The Murrays were packing up to return and get their women and children and celebrate their victory. The Camerons just wandered off without so much as a word, still visibly confused about why they were even there. It didn't appear they would pose so much of a threat as they had been to the Murrays. The MacEacharnas had gathered up Harold's charred remains and were now burning them.

"Wait," Ellie told the others. "I need tae say 'God be with ye' tae Harold."

Eoin opened his mouth to answer.

Ciaran beat him to it, taking Nadia's elbow and turning to follow Ellie down the mountain. "They wull be honored. We all should gae."

* * *

After they'd all paid their respects, the MacGregors gathered again on the mountainside.

Baltair had the faerie axe in his hand, and he beckoned the others to come close to him. "We dinna yet ken if ye need tae be in contact with me tae come along, but it could na hurt for ye tae be, aye?"

"Aye," they all said pretty much in unison, crowding around him and making sure they all had a hand on Baltair.

In Harold's book, Ciaran had just closed his eyes and decided where and when he wanted to go, and he was there. So that's what Baltair did. That dizzy feeling came, the one that nauseated him whenever he traveled through time with Eoin before. When it stopped, he opened his eyes. Just as he had wished, they were all in the woods outside Murray castle.

"Now I wish we would've brought the horses," Ellie said at Baltair's side.

He nudged her. "Certies ye jest. 'Tis na far a walk at all. 'Twill dae oor legs good."

They hadn't gotten close to the castle at all when Meehall and Sarah came running out to meet them. "What a fine surprise," Sarah said.

The look on Meehall's face was cautious. "Tae what dae we owe such joy?"

Eoin spoke up. "'Twill be easier tae show than tae explain. Gae and tell whoever ye must that ye wull be gone a few days."

Meehall went into the castle.

Ellie and Nadia gathered around Sarah, and Ellie asked her, "Sae, is marrit life all 'tis cracked up tae be?"

Sarah gave Ellie a smug smile and winked at Nadia. "All that and sae much more." She beamed a smile at Ciaran. "Sae glad I am, tae see ye hale and hearty again!"

Meehall came out with a bag and took Sarah's arm.

They all went back into the woods.

Eoin said, "If I can hold the axe, I wull take us tae pick up Jeffrey and on tae Da and Mither."

Baltair had a moment of trepidation. What if the axe was just as hard to hand over as the halberd? What if the axe had cursed him just as the halberd had cursed Ciaran? He handed the axe to Eoin with ease, though.

Sighing with relief, Baltair found Ellie looking at him intently, her face relaxing at the same time his did. He went over to her and put his arms around her. "Ellie, I ken we are o' two separate waurlds, but I dinna want tae—"

His world started spinning again, interrupting the most important speech he would ever make in his life.

* * *

Ellie was panicking inside. She wasn't ready to talk about going back to her time. He was so darn protective sometimes. She first needed him to know just how much he meant to her, so he wouldn't insist she leave. In order to refocus Baltair, she asked, "Who is Jeffrey?"

Baltair looked over at his big beefy cousin. "Eoin's twin."

Ellie laughed at what had to be a joke, turning and poking Baltair's arm. "Och, dinna be daft. Eoin canna hae a twin. He has twin brothers."

Baltair didn't wink or chuckle, though. No, his face remained neutral while he waited for her to stop. "I ken 'tis passing strange, but aye, Eoin has a twin alsae. Says it was the druids' doing. Making their mither hae two sets o' twins caused their MacGregor father tae hae a fourth-born son, ye ken.

And every fourth-born son belongs tae the druids. 'Tis Eoin."

That made Ellie think.

"Ellie," said Baltair.

She made herself answer, "Aye?" but she couldn't bring herself into the moment, so struck was her mind at the idea of the druids making someone have twins.

"Ellie, we hae na kenned each other but for a few weeks. Howsoever, I hae come tae care for ye, ower this tyme. Wull ye dae me the great honor o' marrying—"

He said more, but the world spun again, making her nauseated and dizzy, not at all inclined to hear.

When things finally settled down, Ellie and her friends were inside a cave. It ended abruptly with a large opening full of cloudy Scottish sky and rough Scottish sea. In the distance over the sea there was an island, green with grass.

"Bide here a moment," Eoin said. "I wull gae and see if 'tis safe for ye tae enter."

Ellie looked at Baltair for an explanation of where they were, scrunching her forehead up and raising her eyebrow to show she was puzzled.

He shrugged looked at her, but with just as puzzled an expression, then pulled her close and held her to him, leaning his head down to whisper in her ear, "I ken ye plan on gang back tae yer tyme once we hae done oor visiting, aye?"

She wanted to put him off a while, to stop the conversation and give herself more time to think. But she didn't see how she could. Ciaran and Nadia were holding each other close, as were Meehall and Sarah.

Only Connell was standing by himself, and Ellie had only just met him. She couldn't talk to Connell and ignore Baltair, but if she was honest with herself, she didn't need to think about it. She knew the answer. She took in a deep breath and prepared to tell it to Baltair.

Eoin came bustling back down the cave, laughing and interrupting what Ellie might have said. "Ye can coome doon tae the throne room." He turned around and waited for them to follow him.

Hurrying them along when they did, Eoin took them down a rough cave that was jagged and difficult to walk on. But after not long at all, it turned into a normal hallway, carved smooth into the stone floor and walls. Only the ceiling was a bit jagged. The walls were carved with what at first appeared to be decorations, but Ellie gasped when she recognized the symbols. This was Celtic writing. The students studied this at Celtic University. She knew a little bit about it herself just from all the items she typed in the secretarial pool.

Ellie couldn't help but stare all around her.

Finally, they went inside a chamber that was as big as her parents' living room, which was sizable for something underground like this. They'd long since left the sunlight from the seaward mouth of the cave, but airflow was abundant from several holes in the walls. Light was abundant as well, from sconces that hung on the walls every 5 feet around the perimeter of the chamber.

Three huge stone thrones stood on one side of the chamber, but that wasn't even the most amazing thing about the room. For next to Eoin stood someone who looked just like him, only not so buff. She could see now what Eoin might have looked like if he hadn't been a bodybuilder. Jeffrey was handsome and approachable, and no wonder these people had hurried to allow Eoin in.

Eoin was speaking to a man wearing a leine. Gesturing at his twin brother Jeffrey, he asked the man, "Can ye spare Friseal a few days, sae we can take him tae visit oor clan?"

The man in the leine stared at the two of them a long time before he spoke. "Aye, I can spare him. 'Tis my great hope and the hope o' all o' us here that someday, we all get together in one big clan gathering."

Ellie looked to Baltair to see if he had any idea what that meant.

Baltair shrugged, and they were all rushing back down first the smooth hallway and then the jagged hallway until they got to the cave mouth, with its view of the huge island.

Eoin turned to see if they had been followed, and then he beckoned them all close to him.

Baltair gathered Ellie closer to him than to his cousin. "Ellie, wull ye be my—"

The world spun round and round, making it impossible to concentrate on anything else. The nausea always took her by surprise when they traveled this way. It was particularly harsh this time, and when she finally came to awareness again, she knew exactly why. She recognized where they were.

They had traveled a great distance and gone back to the United States, as well as back to the future, to her time. She knew, because they were standing beside a highway sign and it was in miles instead of kilometers. The highway was blacktop, and she could see modern buildings in the distance.

Straight in front of her, though, perhaps half a mile off this modern highway, were the burlap buildings and colorful banners of a Renaissance faire. Brass fanfares and the cheers of outdoor theatre goers and the distant cries of hawkers built the atmosphere even from afar.

Ellie looked to Baltair for his reaction and was amused to see how surprised he was. When she spoke now in modern times, modern English came out without her having to think about it. That was how the druid time travel magic worked. "Our times are so modern now that we like to reenact the past," she told Baltair. "Eoin and Meehall have told me before that your family run this fair. They know more about the UK from 1500 to 1700 than most anyone else in this time, so I imagine their faire is quite authentic. I've been to some before, and actually that helped me when I first went back in time. I sort of knew what to expect. I know the same can't be true for when you first came forward in time."

He nodded, still staring at all the burlap structures ahead.

She took his hand, and they walked to the faire behind his cousins.

Excited calls went out in the air before they arrived, and when they did get to the gate, nine beaming people rushed out to meet them. They were all dressed in authentic Scottish Highlander kilts and plaid long dresses, from the oldest on down to the children.

Eoin, Connell, and Jeffrey rushed to hug them, and then Connell put his arm around one of the older men and turned to face Ellie and her friends, speaking to the man as he introduced each of them. "Baltair and Ciaran are distant cousins, Da. They are descendents of your brother Dombnall. And these ladies are Nadia and Ellie, who work at Celtic University but who met Ciaran and Baltair in their native environment."

'Native environment' was an odd turn of phrase, but everyone seemed to know he meant Ellie and Nadia had time traveled, because no one commented. All of Connell's family ran forward with open arms to give Baltair and Ciaran and even Nadia and Ellie hugs.

"Lest there be any misunderstanding," Eoin said while Ellie was being hugged by two of the children, "Nadia is Ciaran's wife and part of the family as well."

That did it.

Ellie would show him!

She grabbed Baltair's hand and swung him in a grand dance maneuver, getting everyone's attention. Once they were all looking and listening, she met

Baltair's eyes and said in a loud voice, "Yes, Baltair. Yes, I will do you the honor of marrying you!"

Baltair's face lit up with joy as he moved in to kiss her soundly while his clan clapped and cheered and shouted "Welcome to the family, Ellie!"

Still smiling congratulations at Baltair, the other forty-something man in Connell's family came forward and shook Baltair and Ciaran by the forearm. "It's a great joy to meet you, Baltair, Ciaran. I am Dall MacGregor, father of Dombnall. I am your great something grandfather. Let's just not figure out how many greats."

Everyone laughed.

Dall held out his arm, and his wife joined him. "This is my Emily, your great again something...."

One by one, Dall introduced his son Tomas and his wife Amber, his son Peadar who was now the same age as Dall because of time travel and his wife Vange, who were the parents of Meehall, Connell, Jeffrey, and Eoin. And Tomas and Amber's small children who couldn't keep still for long: Betty, Bob, and Sue.

Tomas looked around. "Where's Tavish?"

Emily's face grew worried. She directed her stare at Eoin. "What are you not telling us?"

Eoin looked significantly at all the hustle and

bustle of the faire around them. "Let's go somewhere we can discuss this privately."

Dall led them down what looked like an authentic street of a 16th century village, took them inside one of the burlap buildings, and then pulled up the back wall to reveal a camp of modern RVs and recreational trailers. He led them all to the largest trailer and took them inside.

Ellie felt bad about tracking dirt into his clean home. She could imagine Dad yelling at her for it, and then yelling at Mom to clean it up. She shuddered.

But Emily smiled at her. "Don't worry about it. A little dirt pales in importance, next to seeing my family."

Ellie was so touched by this that she hugged Emily, and Emily hugged her in return.

Once they were all seated in the expanded living / dining area, Meehall, Connell, and Friseal nodded to Eoin, who stood and faced his parents and grandparents. "We are no longer sure we can trust Kelsey. She has become so much a Druid—"

One of the bedroom doors opened loudly, making everyone turn their heads to look.

A man who looked just like Tomas appeared in the doorway.

Everyone got up and rushed toward him, squealing in delight.

"Tavish! What a great surprise."

"When did you get here?"

"It's been awhile."

"How long can you stay?"

Tavish greeted his family warmly but with an amount of reservation on his face that puzzled Ellie until he stepped out of the bedroom and revealed that Kelsey was here with him.

The druidess in the family held up her hand and watched with satisfaction as the faerie axe flew into it. And then Kelsey, Tavish, and the faerie axe disappeared into thin air.

* * *

READ THE EXCITING THREE-BOOK CONCLUSION OF Jane Stain's Dunskey Castle Series!

Time of the Fae

Faeries or Druids?

Time for the Clan

Renfaire Druids (Renaissance Fair, Festival, Man)

Druid Magic (Tavish, Seumas, and Tomas)

Celtic Druids (Time of the Celts-Picts-Druids)

Druid Dagger (Leif, Taran, Luag)

Meehall

Ciaran

Baltair

Time of the Fae

See **Jane Stain's Amazon page** for more.

As Cherise Kelley:

Dog Aliens (a cuddly dog story with a happy ending)

High School Substitute Teacher's Guide

Made in the USA
Las Vegas, NV
03 December 2021